THE KINGFISHER TREASURY OF

Witch and
Wizard
Stories

For three wizard people – Diane, Oliver and George
D. B.

KINGFISHER
An imprint of Kingfisher Publications Plc
New Penderel House, 283-288 High Holborn
London WC1V 7HZ
www.kingfisherpub.com

First published by Kingfisher 1996
This edition published by Kingfisher 2004
2 4 6 8 10 9 7 5 3

A CIP catalogue record for this book is available from the British Library

ISBN 0 7534 1041 9

Printed in India

2TR/1004/THOM/MA/115IWF(F)

THE KINGFISHER TREASURY OF
Witch and Wizard Stories

CHOSEN BY DAVID BENNETT

ILLUSTRATED BY JACQUI THOMAS

KINGFISHER

CONTENTS

THE HARE AND THE BLACK AND WHITE WITCH

Lynne Reid Banks

Some shocking news was being whispered about.

A witch had moved into the neighbourhood.

All the respectable, decent people were naturally appalled. A witch! Good grief, anything could happen with a witch for a neighbour! Evil goings-on . . . spells . . . honest folk being changed into goodness knows what!

The hare decided to take action.

There was no secret about where the witch was living. She had bought (with what appeared to be ordinary money) a broken-down old house, which seemed entirely suited to be a witch's home. It was grey and dark and damp-looking; it had lots of sticky-out bits – bay windows, turrets, and so on – topped off with a spire shaped like a witch's hat.

The hare knew the old house well. It had been

empty for years and was practically falling down. So he was very surprised, as he hopped through the big old iron gates, to see that the house looked completely different.

It looked all smart and pleased with itself. It had had a coat of paint. All the brickwork was painted white, and the woodwork – doors, window frames, and so on – was black. There were some designs in black on the white walls, and in white on the black slate roof.

"Those signs must be something dangerous," thought the hare. He closed his eyes and hopped sideways in the hope that they wouldn't have as much power over him.

As a result, he fell into a hole in a flowerbed. Luckily, it wasn't too deep.

He looked up and saw a young man with a spade gazing at him.

"Are you okay?" asked the young gardener.

The hare, feeling silly, jumped out of the hole. "Fine, fine," he said airily. "Hey! Do you work for the witch?"

"Yes," said the boy, continuing with his digging.

"You shouldn't!" said the hare. "Witches can't be trusted!"

"Is that so?" said the boy. "None of 'em?"

"They're all the same!" answered the hare.

The boy turned his back on the hare and began to whistle while he dug. The hare, who found this annoying, went round the back of the house and found himself in the kitchen.

There was a beautiful young girl cooking some soup.

"Don't tell me you're working for the witch, too!" said the hare in shocked tones.

"Why not?" asked the girl.

"Well, I mean . . . ! Goodness gracious grips! She's wicked!"

"Oh, do you think so?" asked the girl, tasting the soup.

"What's she told you to put in that soup, for instance?" asked the hare craftily. "Tadpoles and bat's liver, I bet, stuff like that, eh?"

"Oxtail and onions," said the girl. "Same sort of thing."

It seemed useless to go on trying to warn her.

"Is the witch at home?"

"Yes," said the girl. "I was just going to take her some coffee in her spell room in the cellar."

"You see? You see?" squeaked the hare. "Up to no good! You'd better look out, you'll find yourself turned into a frog, you will!"

"Might be fun to be a frog," said the girl carelessly.

The hare, exasperated, hopped off to find the stairs to the cellar. Soon he was peering around a big oak door with creaking hinges.

The witch was there all right, turning the pages of a huge old book, chewing a pencil, and making notes. She was dressed as a witch should be, in a long cloak and a pointed hat. But nevertheless, the hare gaped at her in astonishment.

Because instead of being a white witch in black clothes, she was a black witch in white clothes.

"This is too much!" he spluttered. "What kind of magic do you do, anyway? Black magic or white magic?"

"A little of each," said the witch.

"I suppose you'll tell me you do black magic to bad people and white magic to good people!" said the hare.

The witch looked at him, puzzled, her finger keeping her place in the book.

"No, no. The other way round," she said.

Quite baffled by this, the hare sat down and thought. This was not at all what he'd expected.

"Could you do a little spell for me?" he asked at last. "Turn me into something . . . ?"

"I understood you were a magic hare," said the witch.

Uh-oh, not good. She knew about him. He'd have to watch himself.

"Well, yes," he said modestly. "But I can just do the odd trick, vanishing and so on. Beginners' stuff."

"I'm normally only asked to do shape changes as a punishment. What would you like to be turned into?" asked the witch.

"A person," said the hare at once.

The witch turned round and a smile lit her black face. She looked very nice indeed when she smiled, which confused the hare even more.

"Now, this is a fun idea," she said. "Let me see. There are plenty of spells in this book for turning people into creatures, but the other way round . . . ! Here's the spell for person-into-hare . . . I've got an idea. Stand still and we'll see if it works."

The hare stood still and the witch read out:

"No more a man who walks upright,

Be though a hare and dance all night!

– That's the right way round. Now then, let me try it backwards:

Tine la snad dna rah a outh eb,

Tire-pu sklaw ooh nam a rom on.

Goodness, what a tongue twister!"

She looked up. And up.

Standing before her was a tall young man with a crew-cut, a snub nose, and very muscly legs. She took off her glasses and goggled at him, then burst out laughing.

"Great stuff! I did it!" the witch cried. "And I've even made you good-looking!"

Just then the girl from the kitchen came in with a mug of coffee. She goggled, too. "Who's that?" she asked in an admiring voice.

"Like him?" asked the witch smugly. "You can have him." She made a gentle gesture with both hands as if pushing them towards each another.

The hare-lad found himself moving in the direction of the girl, and she came to meet him.

She had a breathless, enchanted look. The hare-lad found he had taken her in his arms and kissed her. It felt very, very strange, but he liked it, and was just going to do it again when she pulled back.

"Wait, though!" said the girl. "I'm in love with the gardener. I don't even know you!" And she gave him a little push and ran out of the room.

"Oh dear," said the witch. "It seems there are some spells even my spells can't compete with." And she chuckled and sipped her coffee.

The hare-lad was feeling some things he'd never felt in all his hare life. He didn't have names for them (they were things like jealousy and being put down), but he didn't care for any of them.

"I don't like being a person," he said sulkily. "I want to be a hare again."

"What do you say?" asked the witch.

"Please," added the hare crossly.

So the witch said the spell the right way round, and the next moment the hare found himself at the right height again, down near the ground. He shook himself and did a short dance to make himself feel all hare again.

The black-and-white witch put down her mug and clapped her hands.

"Great dancing, my friend!" she said. "And now, if you don't mind, I must get on."

"Aha!" cried the hare, remembering what he'd come about. "You have to get on with your wicked spells, isn't that it?"

"The one I'm working on at the moment," said the witch, "is a very hard, new one. I'm trying to close up a big hole in the sky. It's a tall order, I can tell you, with millions of people working against me. I suppose all those people would agree with you about it being wicked, or they'd be helping me."

The hare hopped slowly and thoughtfully to the door, and then turned.

"And do you call that black magic or white magic?" he asked.

"Definitely black," said the witch with a great big black-and-white grin.

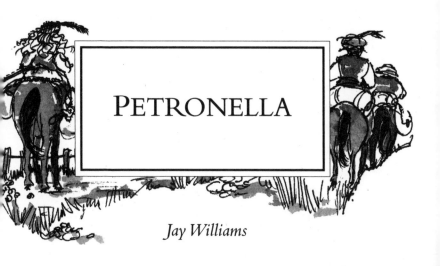

PETRONELLA

Jay Williams

In the kingdom of Skyclear Mountain, three princes were always born to the king and queen. The oldest prince was always called Michael, the middle prince was always called George, and the youngest was always called Peter. When they grew up, they always went out to seek their fortunes. What happened to the oldest prince and the middle prince no one ever knew. But the youngest prince always rescued a princess, brought her home, and in time ruled over the kingdom. That was the way it had always been. And so far as anyone knew, that was the way it would always be.

Until now.

Now was the time of King Peter the twenty-sixth and Queen Blossom. An oldest prince was born, and a middle prince. But the youngest prince turned out to be a girl.

"Well," said the king gloomily, "we can't call her Peter. We'll have to call her Petronella. And what's to be done about it, I'm sure I don't know."

There was nothing to be done. The years passed, and the time came for the princes to go out and seek their fortunes. Michael and George said goodbye to the king and queen and mounted their horses. Then out came Petronella. She was dressed in travelling clothes, with her bag packed and a sword by her side.

"If you think," she said, "that I'm going to sit at home, you are mistaken. I'm going to seek my fortune, too."

"Impossible!" said the king.

"What will people say?" cried the queen.

"Look," said Prince Michael, "be reasonable, Pet. Stay home. Sooner or later a prince will turn up here."

Petronella smiled. She was a tall, handsome girl with flaming red hair and when she smiled in that particular way it meant she was trying to keep her temper.

"I'm going with you," she said. "I'll find a prince if I have to rescue one from something myself. And that's that."

The grooms brought out her horse, she said goodbye to her parents, and away she went behind her two brothers.

They travelled into the flatlands below Skyclear Mountain. After many days, they entered a great dark forest. They came to a place where the road divided into three, and there at the fork sat a little, wrinkled old man covered with dust and spiders' webs.

Prince Michael said haughtily, "Where do these roads go, old man?"

"The road on the right goes to the city of Gratz," the man replied. "The road in the centre goes to the castle of Blitz. The road on the left goes to the house of Albion the enchanter. And that's one."

"What do you mean by 'And that's one'?" asked Prince George.

"I mean," said the old man, "that I am forced to sit on this spot without stirring, and that I must answer one question from each person who passes by. And that's two."

Petronella's kind heart was touched. "Is there anything I can do to help you?" she asked.

The old man sprang to his feet. The dust fell from him in clouds.

"You have already done so," he said. "For that question is the one which releases me. I have sat here for sixty-two years waiting for someone to ask me that." He snapped his fingers with joy. "In return, I will tell you anything you wish to know."

"Where can I find a prince?" Petronella said promptly.

"There is one in the house of Albion the enchanter," the old man answered.

"Ah," said Petronella, "then that is where I am going."

"In that case I will leave you," said her oldest brother. "For I am going to the castle of Blitz to see if I can find my fortune there."

"Good luck," said Prince George. "For I am going to the city of Gratz. I have a feeling my fortune is there."

They embraced her and rode away.

Petronella looked thoughtfully at the old man, who was combing spiders' webs and dust out of his beard. "May I ask you something else?" she said.

"Of course. Anything."

"Suppose I wanted to rescue that prince from the enchanter. How would I go about it? I haven't any experience of such things, you see."

The old man chewed a piece of his beard. "I do not know everything," he said, after a moment. "I know that there are three magical secrets which, if you can get them from him, will help you."

"How can I get them?" asked Petronella.

"Offer to work for him. He will set you three tasks, and if you can do them you may demand a reward for each. You must ask him for a comb for your hair, a mirror to look into, and a ring for your finger."

"And then?"

"I do not know. I only know that when you rescue the prince, you can use these things to escape from the enchanter."

"It doesn't sound easy," sighed Petronella.

"Nothing we really want is easy," said the old man. "Look at me – I have wanted my freedom, and I've had to wait sixty-two years for it."

Petronella said goodbye to him. She mounted her horse and galloped along the third road.

It ended at a low, rambling house with a red roof. It was a comfortable-looking house, surrounded by gardens and stables and trees heavy with fruit.

On the lawn, in an armchair, sat a handsome

young man with his eyes closed and his face turned to the sky.

Petronella tied her horse to the gate and walked across the lawn.

"Is this the house of Albion the enchanter?" she said.

The young man blinked up at her in surprise.

"I think so," he said. "Yes, I'm sure it is."

"And who are you?"

The young man yawned and stretched. "I am Prince Ferdinand of Firebright," he replied. "Would you mind stepping aside? I'm trying to get a suntan and you're standing in the way."

Petronella snorted. "You don't sound like much of a prince," she said.

"That's funny," said the young man, closing his eyes. "That's what my father always says."

At that moment the door of the house opened. Out came a man dressed all in black and silver. He was tall and thin, and his eyes were as black as a cloud full of thunder. Petronella knew at once that he must be the enchanter.

He bowed to her politely. "What can I do for you?"

"I wish to work for you," said Petronella boldly.

Albion nodded. "I cannot refuse you," he said. "But I warn you, it will be dangerous. Tonight I will give you a task. If you do it, I will reward you. If you fail, you must die."

Petronella glanced at the prince and sighed. "If I must, I must," she said. "Very well."

That evening they all had dinner together in the enchanter's cosy kitchen. Then Albion took Petronella out to a stone building and unbolted its door. Inside were seven huge black dogs.

"You must watch my hounds all night," said he.

Petronella went in, and Albion closed and locked the door.

At once the hounds began to snarl and bark. They bared their teeth at her. But Petronella was a real princess. She plucked up her courage. Instead of backing away, she went towards the dogs. She began to speak to them in a quiet voice. They stopped snarling and sniffed at her. She patted their heads.

"I see what it is," she said. "You are lonely here. I will keep you company."

And so all night long, she sat on the floor and talked to the hounds and stroked them. They lay close to her, panting.

In the morning Albion came and let her out. "Ah," said he, "I see that you are brave. If you had run from the dogs, they would have torn you to pieces. Now you may ask for what you want."

"I want a comb for my hair," said Petronella.

The enchanter gave her a comb carved from a piece of black wood.

Prince Ferdinand was sunning himself and working at a crossword puzzle. Petronella said to him in a low voice, "I am doing this for you."

"That's nice," said the prince. "What's 'selfish' in nine letters?"

"You are," snapped Petronella. She went to the enchanter. "I will work for you once more," she said.

That night Albion led her to a stable. Inside were seven huge horses.

"Tonight," he said, "you must watch my steeds."

He went out and locked the door. At once the horses began to rear and neigh. They pawed at her with their iron hooves.

But Petronella was a real princess. She looked closely at them and saw that their coats were rough and their manes and tails full of burrs.

"I see what it is," she said. "You are hungry and dirty."

She brought them as much hay as they could eat, and began to brush them. All night long she fed them and groomed them, and they stood quietly in their stalls.

In the morning Albion let her out. "You are as kind as you are brave," said he. "If you had run from them they would have trampled you under their hooves. What will you have as a reward?"

"I want a mirror to look into," said Petronella.

The enchanter gave her a mirror made of silver.

She looked across the lawn at Prince Ferdinand. He was doing exercises leisurely. He was certainly handsome. She said to the enchanter, "I will work for you once more."

That night Albion led her to a loft above the stables. There, on perches, were seven great hawks.

"Tonight," said he, "you must watch my falcons."

As soon as Petronella was locked in, the hawks began to beat their wings and scream at her.

Petronella laughed. "That is not how birds sing," she said. "Listen."

She began to sing in a sweet voice. The hawks fell silent. All night long she sang to them, and they sat like feathered statues on their perches, listening.

In the morning Albion said, "You are as talented as you are kind and brave. If you had run from them, they would have pecked and clawed you without mercy. What do you want now?"

"I want a ring for my finger," said Petronella.

The enchanter gave her a ring made from a single diamond.

All that day and all night Petronella slept, for she was very tired. But early the next morning, she crept into Prince Ferdinand's room. He was sound asleep, wearing purple pyjamas.

"Wake up," whispered Petronella. "I am going to rescue you."

Ferdinand awoke and stared sleepily at her. "What time is it?"

"Never mind that," said Petronella. "Come on!"

"But I'm sleepy," Ferdinand objected. "And it's so pleasant here."

Petronella shook her head. "You're not much of a prince," she said grimly. "But you're the best I can do."

She grabbed him by the wrist and dragged him out of bed. She hauled him down the stairs. His horse and hers were in a separate stable, and she saddled them quickly. She gave the prince a shove, and he mounted. She jumped on her own horse, seized the prince's reins, and away they went like the wind.

They had not gone far when they heard a tremendous thumping. Petronella looked back. A dark cloud rose behind them, and beneath it she saw the enchanter. He was running with great strides, faster than the horses could go.

"What shall we do?" she cried.

"Don't ask me," said Prince Ferdinand grumpily. "I'm all shaken to bits by this fast riding."

Petronella desperately pulled out the comb. "The old man said this would help me!" she said. And because she didn't know what else to do with it, she threw the comb on the ground. At once a forest rose up. The trees were so thick that no one could get between them.

Away went Petronella and the prince. But the enchanter turned himself into an axe and began to chop. Right and left he chopped, slashing, and the trees fell before him.

Soon he was through the wood, and once again Petronella heard his footsteps thumping behind.

She reined in the horses. She took out the mirror and threw it on the ground. At once a wide lake spread out behind them, grey and glittering.

Off they went again. But the enchanter sprang into the water, turning himself into a salmon as he did so. He swam across the lake and leaped out of the water on to the other bank. Petronella heard him coming – thump! thump! – behind them again.

This time she threw down the ring. It didn't turn into anything, but lay shining on the ground.

The enchanter came running up. And as he jumped over the ring, it opened wide and then snapped up around him. It held his arms tight to his body, in a magical grip from which he could not escape.

"Well," said Prince Ferdinand, "that's the end of him."

Petronella looked at him in annoyance. Then she looked at the enchanter, held fast in the ring.

"Bother!" she said. "I can't just leave him here. He'll starve to death."

She got off her horse and went up to him. "If I release you," she said, "will you promise to let the prince go free?"

Albion stared at her in astonishment. "Let him go free?" he said. "What are you talking about? I'm glad to get rid of him."

It was Petronella's turn to look surprised. "I don't understand," she said. "Weren't you holding him prisoner?"

"Certainly not," said Albion. "He came to visit me for a weekend. At the end of it, he said, 'It's so pleasant here, do you mind if I stay on for another day or two?' I'm very polite and I said, 'Of course.' He stayed on, and on, and on. I didn't like to be rude to a guest and I couldn't just kick him out. I don't know what I'd have done if you hadn't dragged him away."

"But then − " said Petronella, "but then − why did you come running after him this way?"

"I wasn't chasing him," said the enchanter. "I was chasing you. You are just the girl I've been looking for. You are brave and kind and talented, and beautiful as well."

"Oh," said Petronella. "I see."

"Hmmm," said she. "How do I get this ring off you?"

"Give me a kiss."

She did so. The ring

vanished from around Albion and reappeared on Petronella's finger.

"I don't know what my parents will say when I come home with you instead of a prince," she said.

"Let's go and find out, shall we?" said the enchanter cheerfully.

He mounted one horse and Petronella the other. And off they trotted, side by side, leaving Prince Ferdinand of Firebright to walk home as best he could.

GOLD

Ruth Manning-Sanders

Once upon a time there was a young man who owned a small tumbledown farm. He lived alone, far from any village, and about a mile from a sheet of water called the Green Lake.

Well, one autumn evening, an old fellow wearing a ragged black cloak, and carrying an empty sack, knocked at this farmer's door.

"Friend," said he, "may I crave a night's lodging?"

"Surely!" said the farmer. "Step in."

The old fellow in the ragged black cloak stepped in. The farmer set supper before him, and afterwards took him to a small room where there was a bed; and there he slept.

In the morning, the old fellow rose early.

"Friend," said he, "I must go on my way. As you see, I am poor and ragged. I have nothing to offer you but my blessing; and that you shall have." Then he took up his empty sack and walked off towards the Green Lake.

The farmer never gave the old fellow another thought. But during the year that followed, everything prospered with him. His cattle were sleeker and glossier than they had ever been before; his cows gave twice as much milk, and that milk was thick with cream; and every ewe in his little flock bore twins. The farmer put money by, and was able to repair his tumbledown farm.

Next autumn, exactly a year to the day, the old fellow in the ragged black cloak knocked at the farmer's door again, and again asked for a night's lodging. The farmer was able this time to give him a better supper and a better bed. And in the morning the old fellow blessed him again, picked up his empty sack, and walked off towards the Green Lake.

Again for a year the farmer prospered exceedingly. His flocks and herds increased; he bought more land, and was able to hire labourers to help him, and a housekeeper to look after him. "I am indeed greatly blessed!" he thought.

And then he remembered the old fellow in the ragged black cloak, and how he had said, "I leave you my blessing." "Who can he be?" he wondered. "And will he come again?"

The old fellow in the ragged black cloak did come again. He came on an autumn evening as he had done before. And as before he asked for a night's lodging. The farmer bade him welcome, and told his housekeeper to provide the very best supper she could. And when supper was over, he leaned across the table and said, "Friend, who and what are you?"

"A blessing to those whom I bless, and a curse to those whom I curse," answered he of the ragged black cloak.

The farmer felt frightened. "Surely this man must be a wizard," he thought. And he asked no more questions.

But in the morning, when the old fellow had bidden him goodbye and blessed him, and taken up his sack and gone on his way towards the Green Lake, the farmer followed – for he was overcome with curiosity. Near the lake was a fountain, and under the fountain was a wooden trough into

which the spring from the fountain was running. And not far from the wooden trough was a little thicket of alder trees.

And the farmer hid himself in the thicket and watched.

The old fellow in the ragged black cloak went to the trough, lifted a stone slab which covered it, plunged his hands into the water, and began drawing out of it something that looked like bright sand. He filled his sack with the sand; and when the sack was full, he put the stone slab back over the trough, hoisted the sack on to his shoulder, and walked away.

The farmer, peeping through the alders, watched him walking away and away: round by the lake, and through the valley, and up over a grassy hill. He watched till the old fellow became a tiny speck in the distance; he watched till he could see him no more; and then he came out of the alder thicket.

"There must be some value in that sand," he said to himself, "or the old fellow wouldn't come so far to fetch it again and again."

And he went over to the trough, lifted the stone slab and plunged his hands into the water to pick up what lay beneath it.

Heavens above! It was not sand – it was gold dust!

The farmer ran home, took a shovel and the largest sack he could find, and hastened back to the trough. He shovelled up gold dust till the sack was bursting full, and was so heavy that he could barely lift it. Then he dragged the sack into the alder thicket, and hid it.

All that day he could do no work at all for thinking of his sack of gold. When night came, and his housekeeper had gone to bed, he tiptoed out to the stable, bridled his stoutest horse, and rode down to the Green Lake. In the alder thicket it was pitch dark, but the farmer groped about, found his sack, and puffing and panting under its weight, hoisted it on to his horse's back. Then he led the horse to the farm, hid the sack under a pile of straw in the stable, and went to bed – to lie awake all night thinking of his treasure.

In the morning he told his housekeeper that he had a sackful of good grain to spare, and that he was going to the capital of the country to sell it. And so, with his sack of gold strapped on to the back of one horse, and himself riding another, he set off.

It took him three days to reach the capital, and by the time he reached it he was worn out; for he had not been able to sleep at the inns where he put up, for worrying lest someone should discover what was in his sack, and steal it. But no one did steal it.

In the city he sought out the richest merchant, had the sack carried into the office behind the merchant's shop, and, when the door was closed and he and the merchant were alone together, he opened the sack and offered the gold for sale.

"My good man!" said the merchant, "I have not enough money in the world to buy all this gold! Nor, I am sure, have any of my fellow merchants. You must go down the street to that large house at the corner. It is shut up and looks as if nobody lives there. But knock, and the richest man in the country will let you in. Perhaps he will buy your gold – but I cannot be certain. He is a man of strange whims."

So the farmer fastened up his sack again, and the merchant sent two servants with him to carry the sack to the large house at the corner of the street.

The house certainly did look as if no one lived there: every window was closed, every shutter drawn. But when the farmer reached it, he heard a voice calling from somewhere inside, "Farmer, bring here your gold! Open the door and come in."

The farmer opened the door and went in. The servants put down the sack of gold inside the door and went away. The farmer gazed round him in amazement. What splendour, what riches! He was in a great hall hung with cloth of gold and glittering with jewels, and the stairway that wound up at the back of the hall seemed to be cut out of one huge rainbow-coloured crystal.

"Farmer, come up!" called the voice.

The farmer tiptoed up the stairs, and saw before him a door of many coloured jasper.

"Farmer, come in!" called the voice.

The farmer went in through the door. Now he was in a round room that glimmered like a pearl. It had a silver dome, and from the dome hung a crystal lamp burning with a milky flame which sent out sweet odours. But the farmer had no eyes for all this splendour – for there, on a golden throne under the lamp, sat he of the black ragged cloak. But he was not now wearing the black ragged cloak; he was dressed in a rich robe patterned with suns, moons and stars, and on his head was a pointed hat blazing with jewels. His hands were on his knees, and between his hands was a large crystal globe.

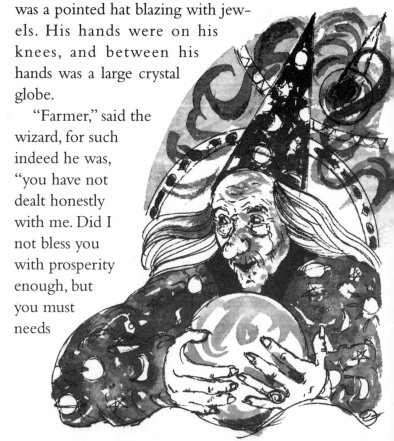

"Farmer," said the wizard, for such indeed he was, "you have not dealt honestly with me. Did I not bless you with prosperity enough, but you must needs clear out my trough? The gold that you have brought me is my own; and as my own I keep it. But since you have three times fed and sheltered me, I will pay you for your three days' journey. Yes, I have watched you every step of your way, and your way has been an anxious one. Here are three pieces of gold for you: one piece for each day's journey. Come, stand by me and look into my globe. I will show you your journey home."

The trembling farmer stepped up to the wizard's side, and looked down into the globe. The globe seemed to be full of clouds, that gathered and parted and gathered again.

"Look steadily," said the wizard. "The clouds will pass."

The farmer looked steadily, and the clouds vanished. There, small, but very bright and clear, he saw a sandy-coloured road winding away out of the city, now between cornfields, now up wooded hills, now down into green valleys. And he saw, travelling along that road, the figure of a man who rode one horse and led another. The man was himself. He saw the man that was himself enter a village, put up at an inn, sup and go to bed, to sleep soundly untroubled by fear of thieves. He saw the whole of his three days' journey home.

And then he saw his farm, with labourers reaping in the fields, and his housekeeper busy in the kitchen. He saw, too, the Green Lake, lying in the valley below his farm; but he saw neither fountain nor trough. Where they had been, a bright stream bubbled up out of the ground and flowed into the lake. Then everything faded; and in the globe he saw only the swiftly moving clouds, gathering and parting, and gathering again.

"Now go home, farmer," said the wizard. "You will never see my fountain or my trough again. I am saving you from further temptation. But work hard, and you shall continue to prosper. I will remain a blessing to you, not a curse."

Without a word the farmer went out of the wizard's house, paid his score at the inn, took his two horses, and rode thoughtfully home. With the three pieces of gold that the wizard had given him, he paid for his three nights' lodging on the way. When he reached his farm, his pockets were empty, but his heart was light.

The wizard never came to visit him again; nor, when he went down to the Green Lake, was there any sign of the fountain or the trough. There was only the bright little stream bubbling up out of the ground and flowing into the lake. He never told a soul about his adventure; but he worked hard, and he continued to prosper, as the wizard had promised. He married a buxom country lass, and by and by had a houseful of merry children.

And all went well with him to his life's end.

THE MEAN PEAR SELLER

Floella Benjamin

Once upon a time, in China, it was customary for traders to set up their stalls outside the gates of large cities where they would sell their wares to passing travellers.

One such trader was a pear seller. He was a very mean man and would charge the hungry travellers high prices for his juicy pears. At the end of the day, as the city gates were about to close, a crowd of poor people would gather around the stalls and the traders would give them any fruit or vegetables that had not been sold, but the pear seller never gave anything away.

One day, as the pear seller sat by his stall, he noticed an old man standing looking at him. The old man was dressed in rags and was obviously very poor.

"Please give me a pear," said the old beggar.

41

"Go away, you filthy old man. If you want a pear, then you must pay for it like anyone else," said the pear seller.

"But I have no money; all I ask for is one pear. I have not eaten all day," replied the beggar.

At this, the pear seller became very angry because the old man was beginning to attract a crowd. "Go away, I tell you!" he shouted. "If I gave every beggar a pear I would soon be poor myself."

Now, standing in the crowd was a young man, who, although poor himself, felt sorry for the old man. "Here you are, old friend," he said, tossing him a coin. "I'll pay for your pear."

The old man picked up a pear and ate it. When he had finished, he said to the young man, "Thank you for your kindness, young sir. Now please allow me to show my gratitude."

At this, he took a pip from the core of the pear and threw it to the ground. The crowd watched as he covered it with earth and spoke a few words under his breath.

Almost at once a small green shoot appeared. It grew rapidly, and within a few minutes it had become a small pear tree laden with ripe, juicy fruit. The crowd of onlookers clapped and cheered with admiration at the old beggar's magical tree and were even more delighted when he told them to help them-selves to the fruit.

When all the pears were picked, the tree disappeared back into the ground as quickly as it had arrived.

Now, all this time the mean pear seller had been watching the display of magic, and he thought of a way he might be able to profit from it. As the crowd of people dispersed, shaking their heads in amazement and carrying armfuls of pears home, he went over to the old man, who was sitting by the roadside, smiling to himself.

"Oh, wise old wizard," said the crafty trader, "you have taught us all a lesson here today. You proved that it is best to be kind and charitable, for anyone who is will be rewarded tenfold."

"That is correct," said the old man. "You have learnt the lesson well."

The cunning pear seller looked humbly at the ground and said, "Then perhaps you could show me the trick, so that I may teach others the same lesson."

At this, the old beggar laughed out loud. "Take a look at your stall, pear seller! It looks as though you do not need tricks to show people the meaning of kindness."

When the mean pear seller looked at his stall, he saw that there was not a single pear left on it. You see, the old man's magic had only made the crowd think they had seen a pear tree grow from a pip – the pears were really from the mean pear seller's stall.

The rest was just an illusion . . . .

THE BOY WITH TWO SHADOWS

Margaret Mahy

There was a little boy who took great care of his shadow. He was quite a careful little boy with his buttons and shoes and all the odd pieces. But most especially he was careful with his shadow because he knew he had only one, and it had to last him his life. He always tried to manage things so that his shadow didn't trail in the dust, and if he just couldn't keep it out of the dust he hurried to get to a clean place for it.

This boy took such care of his shadow that a witch noticed it. She stopped the boy on his way home from school.

"I've been watching you," she said. "I like the way you look after your shadow."

"Well," said the boy, trying to sound grown-up, "the way I see it is this – it's the only one I've got. And it's going to have to last me a long time."

45

"True! True!" said the witch, looking at him with great approval. "You're the lad for me. The thing is, I want someone to look after my shadow while I am away on holiday. I don't want to drag that skinny old thing around with me. You know what a nuisance a shadow can be."

"Mine isn't any trouble," said the boy doubtfully.

"That's as may be," the witch declared. "The thing is, I want to be rid of mine for two weeks, but I'm not going to leave it with just anybody – it's going to be left with you."

The boy didn't like to argue with a witch.

"All right," he said, "but hurry back, won't you?"

The witch bared her teeth in a witch smile, which was quite wicked-looking, though she was trying to be pleasant.

"If you return my shadow in good condition," she promised, "you shall have a magic spell all of your own. I'll choose just the right one for you." Then she fastened her shadow onto the boy's

shadow, got on her broom, and made off, light and free as thistledown, with sunlight all around her and no bobbling black patch chasing at her heels.

The boy now had two shadows. One was his own. The other was the fierce, crooked, thorny shadow of the witch.

The boy had nothing but trouble with that witch's shadow. It was the worst-behaved shadow in the world! Usually, it is a rule that shadows behave much as their people do – but the witch's wouldn't do that. When the little boy went to buy apples the witch's shadow rummaged among the shadows of the fruit. It put the shadows of all the oranges over beside the bananas, and mixed up the shadows of the peaches. Everything was all higgledy-piggledy.

The man in the fruit shop said, "Throw that shadow out! How on earth am I going to sell oranges when they've got no shadows? And who's going to buy bananas with the shadows of oranges?"

The little boy didn't like to turn the witch's shadow loose on its own. He rushed out of the shop without his apples.

At home, all through tea, the witch's shadow stretched itself long and leaped all over the wall. It took the shadow from the clock, and the clock stopped. Then it terrified the parrot into fits, and pulled the shadow-tail of the dog's shadow.

"Really!" said the little boy's mother. "I can't enjoy my tea with that ugly thing waltzing around the walls! You'll have to keep it outside."

But the boy was determined to look after the witch's shadow. From then on, he had his tea in the kitchen on his own. He got so clever at keeping the witch's shadow from getting into mischief and wickedness that at last it couldn't find anything wicked to do. Naturally this made it very cross.

Then suddenly, in spite of the little boy's care, the shadow thought of something new and mean – so mean that you would think even a witch's shadow would be ashamed. It started to pinch and tease and bite and haunt the little boy's own shadow. It was terrible to see. The boy's shadow had always been treated kindly. His own shadow did not know what to do now about this new, fierce thing that tormented it, pushed it onto dusty places and trod on its heels as they hurried down the road.

One day the boy's shadow could bear this no longer. In broad daylight the boy, going home to lunch, saw his two shadows – short and squat – running beside him. He saw the witch's shadow nip his own smaller shadow with her long witch fingernails. His own shadow gave a great bound and broke away from his feet. Down the road it flew, like a great black beetle or a bit of waste paper flapping in the wind, then it was gone. The little boy ran after it, but it was nowhere to be seen. He stood still and listened to the warm summer afternoon. It was so quiet he could hear the witch shadow laughing – or rather, he heard the echo of laughing. (Because, as you know, an echo is the shadow of a sound, and sometimes the sound of a shadow.)

Well, you can just imagine. There was the little boy with only one shadow again – but it was the

49

wrong shadow. His real shadow was quite gone, and now he had only the witch's left.

It was more like having a thorn bush at his heels than a proper shadow. There was nothing comfortable about this, and people stared and nudged one another.

As for the boy, he felt sad and lonely without his own shadow. He tried to like the witch's shadow, and he tried hard to take good care of it – but it was a thankless task. You might just as well try to pet a wild she-wolf or a thistle!

At last the witch came back. She wrote the boy a letter in grey ink on black paper, telling him to meet her that night at midnight and to be sure to bring her shadow with him. (Thank goodness it was a bright moonlit night or it might have been extremely difficult to find that wretched shadow, which hid away from him sometimes.) As it was, the witch whisked it back in half a minute less than no time. (In fact, it didn't even take her as long as that.)

"Now," the witch said very craftily, "here's your

spell." She handed the boy a small striped pill, wrapped in a bat's wing.

"It's one I don't use much myself," she said. "But the boy who swallows that pill can turn himself into a camel. Any sort of camel, even a white racing camel – or a Bactrian or any sort of camel you like."

The little boy couldn't help feeling it was a bit useless, in a way, to be able to turn himself into a camel. What he really wanted was just his own shadow back. He pointed out to the witch that her fierce shadow had driven his own gentle one away. The witch sniggered a bit in a witch-like, but very irritating, fashion.

"Well, my dear,' she said, "you can't expect everything to be easy, you know. Anyhow, I feel I've paid you handsomely for your trouble. Run off home now."

The boy had to do what he was told. He scuttled off sadly down the street to his home, carefully holding down the pocket where he had put the striped pill. It was bright moonlight and everything had its shadow – the trees trailed theirs out over the road, the fence posts pointed theirs across the paddocks. The sleeping cows had sleeping shadows tucked in beside them. Only the little boy had no shadow. He felt very lonely.

At the gate to his house, he thought at first that his mother was waiting for him. A dim figure seemed to be watching out, peering up the road. But it wasn't tall enough to be his mother, and besides, when he looked again it wasn't there. Then something moved without any sound. He looked again. Softly and shyly as if it was ashamed of itself, his own shadow slid out from among the other shadows, and sidled toward him. It slipped along, toe-to-toe with him, just as it had always done.

The little boy thought for a moment:

He was free of the witch's shadow.

He had a magic trick that would turn him into any sort of camel he liked – if he ever wanted to.

And now he had his own shadow back again!

Everything had turned out for the best. He was so pleased he did a strange little dance in the moonlight, while, toe-to-toe, his shadow danced beside him.

THE NOT-VERY-NICE PRINCE

Pamela Oldfield

Prince Ferdinand was not very nice and hardly anybody liked him. Only the Princess Eglantine could put up with his rude manners, and they would visit each other from time to time for a game of Snakes and Ladders.

One day the Prince was driving home in the royal coach when it came to a sudden halt. An old woman was crossing the road with an ancient pram laden with firewood.

The Prince put his head out of the window and shouted at her. "I say, old woman, move that flipping pram out of my way and look sharp about it."

The old woman looked at him. She was very ugly indeed and in need of a good wash.

"Hang on a minute, your Highness," she croaked. "This nearside wheel's a bit wobbly . . . ."

Now a gentleman would have offered to help her but Prince Ferdinand was no gentleman.

"Don't bother me with your excuses," he shouted. "Get the flipping thing out of my way."

Well, the ugly old woman was really a witch. She didn't like his manners and decided to teach him a lesson. She pointed at him with a long bony finger and muttered some magic words. He heard the word "flipping" but that was all.

At once the "flipping thing" flipped. To Ferdinand's dismay the pram rose into the air and turned right over. All the firewood fell out on to the startled horses.

They were very frightened and promptly ran away and the coach came unhitched and rolled into the hedge. The Prince climbed out of his wrecked coach and looked for the old woman but she had disappeared. He didn't know that she had put a spell on him.

But the next day a girl came to the door with a basket of eggs.

"Good day to your Highness," she said politely. "Will you buy some new-laid eggs?"

"No, I won't," he said, without even a thank you.

"But they are beautiful brown eggs," she said.

"They may be sky-blue pink for all I care," he said. "Take the flipping things away."

You can guess what happened!

The basket rose up into the air and turned over. The eggs fell on the Prince's best velvet coat and ruined it.

"Now I see it all!" he cried fearfully. "The old woman was a witch and she has put a spell on me.

I shall have to be very careful what I say from now on."

The Not-Very-Nice-Prince walked about all next day with his hand clapped over his mouth so that he wouldn't say anything foolish . . . but the next morning he forgot again. When the maid carried in his breakfast he sat up in bed and scowled.

"What on earth is that?" he asked.

"Crunchy Pops, your Highness."

"Crunchy Pops!" he grumbled. "I wanted eggs and bacon. Take the flipping things – Ooh!"

Too late he realized what he'd said. The bowl of Crunchy Pops floated into the air and flipped right

over. It emptied itself all over his head. Prince Ferdinand screamed with rage and the terrified maid fled into a nearby broom cupboard and wept copiously.

After that, things went from bad to worse. The Prince became very flustered and that made him even more forgetful. On Monday he flipped a royal banquet.

On Tuesday it was a market stall.

On Wednesday it was a troop of the King's best soldiers!

But he had finally gone too far.

"Get out of my sight," roared the King, stamping his foot so hard that it hurt. Don't come back until the spell is lifted."

Notices were put up warning people to keep away from the Prince and they didn't need telling twice.

So the unfortunate Ferdinand retired to a dark dungeon below the palace and wondered what he should do. He didn't tell anyone where he was and no one bothered to find out – which was very sad.

One day the Princess Eglantine visited the King for a game of croquet. She had almost won the game

when she caught sight of the Prince watching
them from the dungeon. Kindly, she offered to visit
him for a game of Snakes and Ladders.

"How can I concentrate on Snakes and Ladders
at a time like this?" he wailed. "All I need is a
flipping princess who −"

He had done it again! Slowly the Princess rose
into the air and turned over.

She came down on her bottom and everyone
laughed.

The Princess was mortified. "I shall be back

when the spell is lifted and not before," she told the King, and stomped off home with her nose in the air.

The only question was – who could lift the spell? The only visitor to the dark dungeon was an old woman who took him bread and water each day. Prince Ferdinand was so busy feeling sorry for himself he didn't even recognize her. He had plenty of time to ponder his manners and vowed that if the spell were ever lifted he would be a reformed character.

One day the old woman, who was really the witch, came into the dungeon. She had a pail of water and a scrubbing brush and she began to scrub the floor. The Prince looked at her kindly.

"That is hard work for an old woman," he said politely. "Please let me help you."

To the old woman's dismay he seized the scrubbing brush and fell to scrubbing the dungeon floor. She stared at him in horror.

"You nincompoop!" she roared. "You numbskull! Why do you have to be so polite? Your

61

YASHKA AND
THE WITCH

Stephen Corrin

On the edge of a forest, beside a lake, lived a poor woodcutter and his wife. They had no children and this made them very sad. The wife was forever grieving that she had no baby to rock in the cradle, no baby to sing to and care for.

One fine day her husband went into the forest, chopped a nice round log from a tree and brought it home to his wife.

"Rock that," he said.

The wife put the log in the cradle and began to rock it and as she rocked she sang,

Rock-a-bye, rock-a-bye, my little one,
In my little cradle sleeps my darling son.

She went on rocking in this way for one whole day, and the next, and then on the third day, there in the cradle, she was overjoyed to find not a log but a real live baby boy instead. The parents called their son Yashka and as he grew up he longed for the day when he could go out fishing all by himself, in his own little boat, on the lake which he loved so dearly.

On his seventh birthday he said to his father, "Dear father, would you please make me a boat of gold and a paddle of silver, and when I go fishing on our lake I will bring you back as many fish as ever you may need." So his father built him a little boat of gold and a paddle of silver to go with it, and every day Yashka would go out in his little golden boat with his fishing rod, and paddle to the middle of the lake, and there he would fish the whole day long till the sun went down. At midday, though, his mother would bring him his dinner. She would come to the lakeside, cup her hands and call:

Yashka, my son, your work is half done,
Bring me your fish and eat up this dish.

And Yashka would paddle his boat to the lakeside, give his mother the fish he had caught and eat his dinner.

Now the witch, Baba Yaga, the bony one, lived deep in the forest which surrounded the lake. She had heard Yashka's mother call to him, so one day, just before noon, she took a sack and a long hook, made her way to the edge of the lake and called:

Yashka, my son, your work is half done,
Come bring me your fish and eat up this dish.

So Yashka paddled his boat to the shore, thinking it was his mother calling him, and Baba Yaga hooked her long hook to his boat, dragged it to the bank, seized the boy and pushed him into the sack.

"That's the end of your fishing!" she gloated, rubbing her skinny hands. She slung the sack over her shoulder and trudged back to her hut, deep in the forest. But as the sack was very heavy and the climb to her hut was very steep she sat down to rest. She soon dozed off, snoring a most witch-like snore. Yashka managed to crawl out of the sack, filled it with heavy stones and rushed through the forest back to the lake.

When Baba Yaga woke up she picked up the sack again and carried it to her hut. Inside was her daughter, more hideous than Baba Yaga herself. "There!" said the old crone, "I've bagged a fine one here," and she tipped up the sack . . . and out came tumbling all those heavy stones. Baba Yaga flew into a most frightful rage. Stamping and shrieking and brandishing her besom, she yelled, "I'll show him. He'll not cheat me a second time." Off she flew in her mortar, beating furiously with her pestle and sweeping her tracks with her besom, back to the lake. In a voice that barely concealed her fury she called:

Yashka, my son, your work is half done,
Come bring me your fish and eat up this dish.

"That's not my mother's voice," cried Yashka. "Her voice is not so thick and rough."

"Not so thick, is it?" muttered the witch. "I'll soon make it finer, my boy, never you fear!" And off she flew to the blacksmith.

"Blacksmith, blacksmith," she croaked. "Forge me a voice, a fine voice, a voice as fine as Yashka's mother's." The terrified smith set to work. "Place your tongue on my anvil," he said, and Baba Yaga stuck out her long, monstrous tongue and the smith flattened it on his anvil.

The witch then hurried back to the lake. This time, in a gentle voice, she called:

Yashka, my son, your work is half done,
Come bring me your fish and eat up this dish.

Yashka heard the call and thought it was his mother's. He paddled his boat to the shore. Baba Yaga, hidden in a thicket, quickly sprang out, hooked him in and bundled him into a sack. "You won't get away this time!" she snarled. She dragged poor Yashka in the sack back to her hut and, kicking the door open, she shouted in triumph to her daughter, "Heat up the oven quick, my girl." Then off she swept, while her daughter got everything ready. Yashka hardly dared look at the daughter, so frighteningly ugly was she with her fanged teeth, long hook-like chin and clawing finger-nails. He shuddered, but he kept his wits. The witch-girl brought in a flat shovel. "Lie down on that," she shrieked. Yashka lay down on the shovel but he stuck his legs up in the air. "No, not like that!" screamed Baba Yaga's daughter. "I can't get you into the oven with your legs sticking up!" Yashka then dropped his legs over the side of the shovel. "No, that's no good either!" yelled the daughter.

"Well, you show me how," said Yashka.

"This is how!" she snarled and she lay down on the shovel to show him. Quick as lightning Yashka pushed the shovel with the witch on it into the oven and closed it tight. Out he rushed from the hut and was just in time to leap on to the branch of a tree and hide among the leaves, as Baba Yaga came back into the hut. She called her daughter, but nobody answered and she realized that the boy had somehow escaped yet again. The old crone went black with rage. She rushed straight out of the hut and made for the tree where he was hiding. Blind with fury, she hacked at the tree with her claws and gouged it with her fanged teeth. She gnawed and scraped till she broke her teeth. But the tree held firm.

More frantic than ever, she rushed to the blacksmith.

"Forge me an axe to chop down that tree," she screamed. The trembling smith had no choice but to obey, and when the axe was ready Baba Yaga flew back with it to the tree and tried to hew it down. After several mighty blows the tree leaned over, and just as she dealt a final cut the axe struck against a stone so that its blade became chipped and blunt. At that very moment a flock of geese came flying by.

"Geese! Geese!" cried Yashka, "the bony-legged Baba Yaga is trying to catch me. Please, geese, drop me each a feather so that I can make wings and fly back to my mother and father."

Feathers came flying down towards him and Yashka made them into wings. Baba Yaga, in a frenzy, chopped so hard that the tree came crashing down on top of her and struck her dead.

Yashka flew home, and the geese followed. He landed on the thatched roof of his cottage and was just in time to hear his mother saying to his father, "Let us eat to give us strength. Perhaps today we shall find our darling Yashka. Here is some good hot bortsch for you, my dear."

"And what about some for me?" called Yashka down the chimney.

His parents did not know whether to laugh or cry to see him fly into the cottage with his goose-feather wings. They showed their gratitude to the geese by throwing them lots of the choicest grain and seeds.

As for Yashka, after rejoicing with his parents at his safe homecoming, he went, the following day, in search of his little golden boat. And there it was, just where the witch had left it, with its silver paddle, waiting for Yashka to row it away.

Every day he went fishing on his lake, and caught more than enough fish for them all to live happily to the end of their days.

THE
IMPROVING
MIRROR

Terry Jones

A magician once made a magical mirror that made everything look better than it really was.

It would make an ugly man look handsome, and a plain woman beautiful.

"I will bring happiness to a lot of people with this mirror," said the Magician to himself. And he went to the main city, where he had his invention announced to the public. Naturally everybody was very curious to see themselves more handsome and more beautiful than they really were, and they queued up to see the magical improving mirror.

The Magician rubbed his hands and said: "I will not only make people happy – I will also make my fortune!"

But before he was able to show the mirror to a single person, a most unlucky thing occurred.

It so happened that the King of that particular

country had married a Queen who was bad-tempered, selfish and cruel. The King put up with all her faults of character, however, because she was also very, very beautiful. She also happened to be extremely vain. So when she heard about the improving mirror, she simply couldn't wait to get her hands on it before anyone else.

"But, my dear," said the King, "you know you are already the most beautiful lady in the realm. And I should know – I searched the kingdom through and I found no one whose looks surpassed yours. That's why I married you."

But the Queen replied: "I must see how even more beautiful I can look in this magical mirror." And nothing would satisfy her but to be the first to look in the improving mirror.

So the King sent for the Magician with strict instructions that he was to show the mirror to nobody until he had demonstrated it to Queen Pavona.

Well, the Magician entered the audience chamber with a feeling of dread.

"Great Queen!" he said with a low bow. "You are the most peerless beauty in this land. No one could be more beautiful than you are now. I beg you not to look in my magic mirror!"

But the Queen could not contain her eagerness to see herself in the improving glass, and she said:

"Show me at once! I must see myself even more beautiful than I really am!"

"Alas!" said the Magician. "I made this mirror for those less fortunate in looks – to give them hope of how they might be."

"Show me!" cried Queen Pavona. "Or I will have you executed on the spot!"

Well, the poor Magician saw there was nothing for it but that he must show the Queen the magic improving mirror. So he brought out the special box in which he kept it locked away, but he did so with a heavy heart.

He took the key, which he had tied around his waist, and opened up the lock. The courtiers pressed around, but the King ordered them to stand back, and the box was brought nearer the throne.

Then the Magician lifted the lid, and the Queen peered in. There she saw the magic mirror – lying face down.

"Your Majesty!" said the Magician. "I fear only evil will come of your looking in my magic mirror."

"Silence!" shouted the Queen, and she seized the mirror and held it up to her face.

For some moments she did not speak, nor move, nor even breathe.

She was so dazzled by the reflection before her. If her eyes had been dark and mysterious before, now they were two pools of midnight. If her cheeks had been fair and rosy before, now they were like snow touched by the dawn sun. And if her face had been well-shaped before, now it was so perfect that it would carry away the soul of anyone who gazed upon it.

For what seemed a lifetime, her eyes feasted on the image before her. And everyone in the court waited with bated breath.

Eventually the King spoke: "Well, my dear? What do you see?" he asked.

Slowly the Queen came to her senses. As she did so, the Magician trembled in his shoes, and humbled himself on the floor before her.

"Does it make you more beautiful?" asked the King.

Queen Pavona suddenly hid the mirror in her sleeve, glared around the court and cried: "Of course not! It's just an ordinary mirror! Have this charlatan thrown into the darkest dungeon!"

So the poor Magician was carried off down to the darkest dungeon.

Meanwhile the King turned to Queen Pavona and said: "Perhaps it will work for me, since I am less well favoured than you ..."

"I tell you it's just an ordinary mirror!" cried the Queen. "I shall use it in my chamber."

And with that, she went straight to her room, and hid the magic mirror in her great chest.

Now the truth of the matter is that the moment Queen Pavona had looked into the magic mirror and seen herself even more beautiful than she really was, she had been consumed with jealousy. She could not bear the thought that there was a beauty greater than hers – even though it was that of her own reflection! So she locked the mirror away, resolving that no one should ever look in it again.

None the less, she could not forget what she had seen in that looking-glass, and – despite her resolve – she found herself drawn to it, and time and again she would creep into her room and steal a look in the magic glass. Before long, she was spending many hours of the day alone in her chamber, gazing into that mirror, trying to see what made her reflection so much more beautiful than she already was.

As the weeks passed, Queen Pavona began to try and make herself more like her reflection in the magic looking-glass. But, of course, it was no use. For no matter how beautiful she made herself, her reflection became even more beautiful still.

The more she tried, the more she failed, and the more she failed to be as beautiful as her reflection in the magic mirror, the more time she spent alone in her room, gazing into it. Until eventually she hardly ever came out of her room – not even to eat or to dance or to make merry with the rest of the court.

Meanwhile the King grew more and more anxious about his wife, for she never explained to him what kept her in her room from morn till night, and whenever he entered the chamber, she always took care to hide the magic mirror.

One night, however, after Queen Pavona had been poring all day over her reflection in the fatal looking-glass, she fell asleep with it still in her hand.

It so happened that some time later the King entered her chamber to kiss her goodnight, as was his custom.

The King had, long ago, guessed that the magic mirror was the cause of his wife's strange behaviour, and he too had long been curious to see just what was so special about it. So when he found her fast asleep on her couch, with the magic mirror still in her hand, he couldn't resist. He lifted it slowly to her face and gazed into it. And there he saw for the first time his Queen's reflection in the magic looking-glass.

The King had believed he would never find another woman more beautiful to his sight than Queen Pavona. But now he saw in the magic mirror the reflection of someone who was three times as beautiful, and he let out a cry as if he had been stabbed to the heart.

At that, the Queen woke up with a scream of rage, and she struck the King with the mirror – so hard that he fell over.

"How dare you look in this mirror!" she cried, her face all screwed up with anger. Well, of course, when the King looked at her now with her face distorted by rage, he thought that Queen Pavona was almost ugly compared to her reflection.

"How dare you strike me!" cried the King. And he strode out of the Queen's chamber, resolving that he would put up with her ill-temper no longer.

From that day on, the King scarcely spoke to his Queen, or even set eyes on her. But he could not forget the vision of loveliness that he had seen in the magic glass.

Now all this while, the poor Magician had been languishing in the darkest dungeon. And every day he cursed himself for making the improving mirror.

Then one day, in the midst of his misery, the door of his cell was flung open and in strode the King!

The Magician fell at his feet and cried: "Mercy,

O King! Have you come to release me? You know I've done nothing wrong."

"Well . . . That's as maybe," replied the King. "But if you want to get out of this dungeon, there is something you must do for me."

"Anything that is within my power!" exclaimed the Magician.

"Very well," said the King. "I want you to change the Queen, my wife, for her reflection in your magic looking-glass."

"But Your Majesty!" cried the Magician. "That would be a cruel thing to do to your wife!"

"I don't care!" replied the King. "I am sick of her evil temper, her selfishness and her cruelty. And now I have seen her reflection – which is so much more beautiful than she ever can be – I am no longer even satisfied by her looks. Can you change her for her reflection?"

"Alas!" cried the Magician. "Is this the only way I can gain my freedom?"

"If you can't do it, then you can rot in here until you die – for all I care!" said the King.

"Then I shall do it," said the Magician. "But we shall both suffer for it."

And so the King released the Magician from his dungeon, and the Magician was led into the Queen's chamber.

The Queen was standing as usual in front of the magic glass, staring at her reflection. "What do you want?" she cried as the King entered.

"You wish you were more like your reflection, my dear?" said the King. "Then so do I!"

At which the Magician threw a handful of magic dust into the air, and for a few moments it filled the chamber so that no-one could see.

Then, as the dust cleared, a most extraordinary thing happened.

There was a flash and a groan, and suddenly the mirror rose up into the air – but the Queen's reflection stayed where it was! Then the mirror turned over several times in the air, before landing over the Queen herself.

And so the King had his wish.

From that time on, Queen Pavona's beautiful reflection became his wife, and the real queen was trapped for ever in the mirror. But, just as the Magician had promised, the King lived to regret the change. For even though she was now his wife, the Queen's reflection was still only a reflection, and when the King tried to touch her beautiful skin – he found it was as cold as glass.

What's more, he soon discovered that the Queen's reflection was not only more beautiful than the real Queen, it was also more heartless, more selfish and even more ill-tempered. And many a time he longed for the Magician to change them back.

But the Magician had long since fled the country, and now lived in miserable exile, swearing that he would never make another magic mirror that could so inflame the vanity of those who were already vain enough.

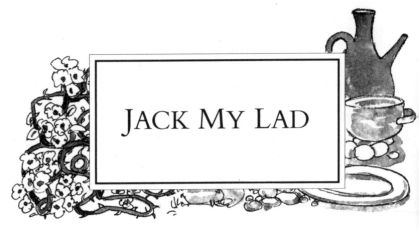

JACK MY LAD

Alan Garner

Jack was a boy that sold buttermilk, and one day, as he went along, he met a witch.

"Jack, my lad," said the witch, "sell me a bit of your buttermilk."

"No," said Jack. "I shall not."

"If you don't," said the witch, "I'll put you in my sack."

"No," said Jack. "Not a drop," said Jack. "You can't have any; and that's that."

So the witch put Jack in her sack, the sack on her back, and set off for home. After a while, she said, "Eh up. I was forgetting. I'll want some fat to fry with."

"Then you'd best let me down, missis," said Jack, "and go fetch your fat. I'm too big to carry to the shop."

"If I do that," said the witch, "you'll run away."

"No, I'll never," said Jack.

The witch saw some men who were cutting a thorn tree; and she said to them, "Just you keep an eye on this sack for me while I go fetch some fat to fry with."

"Right you are, missis," said the men. "We'll keep an eye on your sack."

So the witch left the sack with the men, and off she went to fetch her fat.

As soon as she was gone, "Now then," said Jack. "You let us out, and I'll give you some buttermilk." Well, the men let Jack out, and he gave them some buttermilk, and he said, "I know what. Fill this here sack up with the thorns you've been cutting, and I'll get off home."

So the men filled the sack with the thorns, and Jack went home. And along comes the witch with the fat, takes the sack full of thorns, sets the sack on her back, and off she goes.

Well, it wasn't long before those thorns began to prick her, and the witch, she said, "I reckon you've got pins in your pocket, Jack, my lad. I mustn't forget to take them out when I'm frying." But when she got to her house and opened the sack and tipped the thorns onto a clean white sheet, she said, "Well, I'll be jiggered! Jack, my lad, I'm going to catch you, and then I'm going to boil you; and that's a fact."

The next day, Jack met the witch again.

"Jack, my lad," said the witch, "sell me a bit of your buttermilk."

"No," said Jack. "I shall not."

"If you don't," said the witch, "I'll put you in my sack."

"No," said Jack. "Not a drop," said Jack. "You can't have any; and that's that."

So the witch put Jack in her sack, the sack on her back, and set off for home. After a while, she said, "Eh, up. I was forgetting. I'll want some salt to boil with."

"Then you'd best let me down, missis," said Jack, "and go fetch your salt. I'm too big to carry to the shop."

"If I do that," said the witch, "you'll run away."

"No, I'll never," said Jack.

The witch saw some men who were digging a hole; and she said to them, "Just you keep an eye on this sack for me while I go fetch some salt to boil with."

"Right you are, missis," said the men. "We'll keep an eye on your sack."

So the witch left the sack with the men, and off she went to fetch her salt.

As soon as she was gone, "Now then," said Jack. "You let us out, and I'll give you some buttermilk."

Well, the men let Jack out, and he gave them some buttermilk, and he said, "I know what. Fill this here sack up with the stones you've been digging, and I'll get off home"

So the men filled the sack with the stones, and Jack went home. And along comes the witch with

85

the salt, takes the sack full of stones, sets the sack on her back, and off she goes.

Well, it wasn't long before the stones began to rattle, and the witch, she said, "My lad Jack, your bones do crack!" But when she got to her house and opened the sack and tipped the stones onto a clean white sheet, she said, "Well, I'll be jiggered! Jack, my lad, I'm going to catch you, and then I'm going to roast you; and that's a fact."

The next day, Jack met the witch again.

"Jack, my lad," said the witch, "sell me a bit of your buttermilk."

"No," said Jack. "I shall not."

"If you don't," said the witch, "I'll put you in my sack."

"No," said Jack. "Not a drop," said Jack. "You can't have any; and that's that."

So the witch put Jack in her sack, the sack on her back, and set off for home. And when she got to her house, the witch said to her cat, "Just you keep an eye on this sack for me, while I fetch sticks for the fire."

The witch left the sack with the cat, and locked the door behind her while she fetched sticks for the fire.

As soon as she was gone, "Now then," said Jack. "You let us out, and I'll give you some buttermilk."

Well, the cat let Jack out, and he gave it some buttermilk; and after that, he filled the sack with every pot in the witch's scullery. Then he ran up the flue, down the roof and all the way back to his own house.

The witch came in with the sticks. She lit the fire, opened the sack, tipped the pots onto a clean white sheet, and broke them every single one.

"Well, I'll be jiggered!" said the witch. "Jack, my lad!" she shouted up the chimney. "Keep your buttermilk, you great nowt! And never again come near me!"

And he never did.

THE
FAT WIZARD

Diana Wynne Jones

The Fat Wizard lived up at the Big House in our village and he always opened the Church Fête. As well as being very fat, he had a purple face and pop eyes and a grey bristly beard. He despised everyone. When he opened the Fête, he said things like, "This Fête gets more boring every year. Why do you silly people love it?" This was considered very witty, because the Fat Wizard was rich. I preferred Mrs Ward's cousin Old Ned, myself. Everyone despised Old Ned, but at least he went mad in the church porch every full moon. The Fat Wizard never did anything but grumble.

My Auntie May always went to the Church Fête, although we were Chapel. She went for the jumble. Auntie May was the most respectable witch I have ever known and she did not like Chapel people to know she bought cast-off clothes. She lived in the house on the corner opposite the White Horse and everything indoors was just so. I came to live in that house as soon as I left school, to train to be Auntie May's assistant.

Auntie May used to look through her lace curtains and count how often Mrs Ward went into the pub. "Look at her!" she would snort. "Red dress, hung all over with jewellery, and enough make-up to sink a battleship!" Though they were both witches, Auntie May and Mrs Ward were opposites in every way. Auntie May was tall and lean and dour, and she wore dour brown clothes. Mrs Ward was small and glamorous, and she had lovely legs. I used to admire Mrs Ward and wish I was her assistant, not Auntie May's.

Anyway, the Church Fête was only two days away. Auntie May and I were talking about it while I cleared away breakfast.

"And you're not to bowl for the pig this year, Cheryl," Auntie May was saying, when there was a sort of boom and a flash. The Fat Wizard's manservant George appeared in the middle of the kitchen.

"The Wizard wants to see you at once," George said.

Really, it was a wonder I didn't drop the teapot! Everyone said George was really a demon, but I didn't think even demons had a right to appear in people's kitchens like that.

Auntie May took it quite calmly. "What does he want?" she said. But George only vanished, with another boom and a flash. "Well, we'd better go," Auntie May said, getting her flat brown hat off its peg and pinning it bolt upright across her head.

So off we went, with me wondering what gave the Fat Wizard the right to order us about. As we passed the Vicarage and came to the church, I was wishing for about the thousandth time that I could go and live in Town. The Vicar was trying to chase my pig Ranger out of the churchyard.

"About that pig," Auntie May said forbiddingly.

"I won't do it again," I said guiltily, as we turned into the drive of the Big House. I'd won Ranger at the Church Fête last year, you see, and I'm pretty sure I won him by unfair use of magic. You know how it is, when you're willing and willing for the skittles to fall over. I went a bit far in my willing, and I'm pretty sure half the skittles went over without my bowls even touching them. I was given this squealing, struggling, long-legged piglet, and there was only my mother's tiny backyard to keep him in. He kept getting out. At first, people in the village kept catching him and bringing him back. But he got cleverer and cleverer, until everyone gave up. By now Ranger was a large white amiable pig, and you were likely to meet him anywhere.

The Vicar was still shouting at Ranger as we came to the Big House. George opened the tradesmen's door to us. "Took your time, didn't you?" he said, and he led the way down a corridor, waggling his rump as he walked. I think he waggled because he was allowing for a tail, and he didn't have a tail in human form. But he shocked Auntie May. She whispered to me not to look.

The Fat Wizard was in a sunny morning-room having breakfast. When we came in, he was scraping up the last of a quart tub of fat-free yoghurt. Then he poured a pint of milk on a hill of branflakes, emptied the sugar bowl over it and ate most of that before he looked up. "Here at last, are you, May?" he grunted. He didn't notice me.

"What can we do for you, sir?" Auntie May asked.

The Fat Wizard guzzled up the rest of his branflakes. Then he cut a giant slice off a starch-reduced loaf. He spread that with most of a packet of slimmers' margarine and ladled marmalade on top of that. "The doctors say I'm too fat," he said peevishly. "They make me eat this chicken-feed all the time, but it's not doing a scrap of good. I've got to lose weight. Make me up a potion that will do the trick."

"Of course, sir," Auntie May said politely. "But couldn't you do that yourself, sir?"

The Fat Wizard tipped the rest of the jar of marmalade on his bread and ate it in two bites. "Potions are not men's work," he said with his mouth full. "Go away, woman, and mix me a weight-reducing potion, and get it here today, or I'll get Tallulah Ward to do it."

Rude old man! We hurried home, and Auntie May did her best for him, but it is not easy to set that kind of spell quickly, even when she had me to grind up the ingredients for her. We worked hard the rest of the day. We were straining the mixture all evening, and we only had it bottled just before midnight.

"Take it round to him, Cheryl," Auntie May said breathlessly, slapping a label on the bottle. "And run!"

I supposed Auntie May could not bear the thought of Mrs Ward being asked to do the potion. I took the bottle and set off down the street at a trot, with the bottle foaming and fizzing eerily in my fist. It was quite dark, and I was scared. When I turned in at the gate of the Big House, a large white shape drifted across the drive in front of me. I was too scared even to scream. I just stood.

Then the moon came up over the Fat Wizard's chimneys and the white shape said "Honk!", and I realized it was only Ranger. He knew it was me. He came and brushed his bristly self against me.

"Yes, you're a nice pig," I said. "Much nicer than the Fat Wizard. But don't ever do that again!"

Then I went on and George tried to scare me too. He appeared suddenly in a red light, outside the front door. But I had used up all my fright on Ranger. I held the bottle scornfully out to him. George snatched it. Then he turned and went in through the front door without opening it first, waggling his stern as he melted through it.

I was annoyed, and I could hear Ranger grunting and foraging among the trees as I went back down the drive, so I was not particularly frightened until I got to the gate. Then midnight struck. Something howled, like a dog, but not quite like, over in the churchyard. My hair tried to stand on end, until I realized that it was full moon and the noise was only Old Ned, going mad as usual. I went across the road to have a look.

This is something all the village children like to do. There was a whole row of them sitting on the churchyard wall, ready to watch Old Ned. The biggest was Lizzie Holgate's eldest boy, Jimmy, from the council houses. Jimmy said, "We've been feeding your pig all this week."

"Thanks," I said.

"He's a good animal," Jimmy said. "I like a pig with brains."

"Shut up!" someone else whispered. "Old Ned's starting."

Old Ned came crawling out of the church porch on all fours. That was how he always began. He thought he was a wolf. But I still don't know why they called him *Old* Ned. There was no grey in his hair. When he felt the moonlight across his face, he stood up and stretched both arms in the air.

"Silver temptress!" he shouted. "Take this spell off me!"

We giggled a bit and waited for what he would say next. He can go on for hours. He came shambling down the path between the graves, staring. "I see you!" he yelled. "I see you, Cheryl Watson!"

And he was staring straight at me. I could feel the row of boys moving away from me. Nobody dared be with anyone Old Ned noticed at full moon.

"I see you, Cheryl," said Old Ned. "My mistress tells you to make sure to spend tomorrow night at your mother's house. It will be to your advantage." He gave a mad laugh and went shambling back into the church porch.

"The show's over," Jimmy said to the others. They all got off the wall and ran away without speaking to me. I didn't think the show *was* over. Old Ned began howling again as I went back to Auntie May's, but none of us felt like staying. I kept wondering. I woke up next morning still wondering why Old Ned had noticed me.

But that went out of my head when Mrs Ward came banging on Auntie May's door. Auntie May glared at her. Mrs Ward had her hair in a pink turban and her red coat on over what looked to be a frilly nightdress. Tears were driving black streaks down her make-up.

"Oh, what *have* you gone and done to our poor Fat Wizard!" she gasped. She was killing herself laughing. "Come and take a look!"

We ran outside. Most of the village was out there, either in a row in front of the White Horse or up in the churchyard. And there was George, frantically running up the street with a coil of rope, trying to throw a loop of rope over the Fat Wizard. The Fat Wizard was floating and bobbing about forty feet over everyone's heads. You could see he was nearly as light as air. And he was livid. He was wearing purple pyjamas and his face was the same colour. His eyes were blue bubbles of pure rage.

"Oh dear," said Auntie May.

"It's not your fault," I said. "He asked you to reduce his weight."

"Get me *down*, George!" the Fat Wizard bawled in a high windy voice.

George threw the rope again and hit him with the loop, which made the Fat Wizard bob another ten feet up in the air. The wind caught him and whirled him towards the church.

"Help, George!" he yelled, bouncing against the steeple.

"Trying to, sir! Out of my way!" George shouted, leaping over gravestones and dodging among staring people. "Oh, I do blame myself for opening the window without looking, sir!"

Another gust of wind sent the Fat Wizard slowly bumping and scraping up the steeple. Auntie May went indoors then and made me come too. She said the disgrace was too much. I couldn't see properly from her house. All I could see was Lizzie Holgate arriving, pushing her old pushchair with her twins in it, with Mary and Jimmy and Charlene carrying the smaller babies. I saw Lizzie take two of the babies and send Jimmy and Mary off, but I couldn't see *where*. Jimmy told me later.

The Fat Wizard was hooked on the weathercock by then. But of course George was a demon, so he couldn't touch the church. Lizzie sent Jimmy and Mary up the stairs inside the steeple with the rope. They climbed out at the top and tied the rope to him. Then they unhooked him and George hauled him down into the churchyard. Jimmy said the Fat Wizard didn't even thank them.

While that was happening, Mrs Ward ran past and went into her house, still laughing. Soon after, George came panting along with the rope over his shoulder, towing the bobbing, fluttering Fat Wizard like an angry barrage balloon. We had a good view, because Mrs Ward lived six houses up, beyond the place where the road bends round the White Horse. It took George twenty minutes to work the bouncing and bobbling Fat Wizard through Mrs Ward's front door.

"Well, she should have had time to get dressed by now – even the way she dresses," Auntie May said viciously.

She was very upset. So was I, rather. It could have been my fault. I told you how I came to win Ranger in the heat of the moment. I *could* have put in a bit of ill-wishing when I grated the ingredients or when I handed the potion to George. That made me feel I ought to keep out of Auntie May's way for a while. I asked if I could go and see my mother.

Auntie May felt like being alone. She told me to stay the night if I wanted. "But make sure to come back in time to go to the Fête tomorrow," she added.

My mother lives out along Water Lane. It felt strange to be going there and not living there any more.

"Is someone blaming you for that weight–reducing spell?" my mother asked. She had heard all about it, of course.

"I'm not sure," I said. "Has there been anything to my advantage here?"

"Not that I know of," said my mother.

"Then I'll have to stay the night," I said.

Mother was not too keen on the idea. She turned out to be using my old room as an apple–store. But she is fond of me, and she let me spend the night on the sofa, which was much warmer than my old room. And in the morning, as if Old Ned had *known*, there was a letter from my Godmother. My Godmother is head of the biggest coven in Town. She wrote that I must be about old enough to be leaving school now, and she invited me to come and join her and train to be a witch.

"Wire and tell her you can't," said my mother.

"If I'd known she was going to offer, I'd never have let you go to May. But it's too late now. You can't let May down."

"Bother!" I said sadly. I was longing to live in Town. I put the letter in my pocket to answer later and went back to Auntie May's.

I came back to a sight I had quite often seen before. Auntie May was standing dourly in the street, staring at her house. Most of the side wall was missing. the roof was sagging, the front room was filled with broken laths, plaster and the ruins of Auntie May's furniture. The house is on a right-angled bend, you see. A lorry driver coming through the village in the night could see the White Horse, but not Auntie May's house on the other side of the street beyond it. This lorry driver had not turned his wheel quickly enough and had arrived in Auntie May's front room in the middle of the night. He had driven through my bedroom too. Almost the first thing I saw through the hole was the ruins of my bed, upside down in the plaster next to the street. My bedroom floor was missing. I gulped a bit when I saw and said a silent "Thank you" to Old Ned.

"I am insured," Auntie May said glumly. "And I dare say I deserved it for getting that potion wrong."

"You mean," I said, "the Fat Wizard?"

Auntie May said, "Hush!" and gave a stiff, uneasy look all round. "Yes, this happens every time I cross him. Well, come in. The kitchen's still there."

We picked our way through the rubble. I no longer wondered why Auntie May hurried to obey the Fat Wizard when he wanted something. And I was angry. The Fat Wizard had not even *thought* what might happen to me!

"They say he gave Tallulah Ward a gold bracelet," Auntie May said bitterly, while the kettle boiled. "She made him heavy again. I saw him walk past on his own two feet with that George fussing round him. Ah well, life is not meant to be fair. I mustn't grumble."

I did not agree at all. I said, "Didn't he give the Holgates anything?"

"Of course not!" Auntie May said, surprised at the idea.

I was still angry when we set off to the Church Fête that afternoon. We had to spend all morning putting No Entry spells on the house. The builder was too busy with the Fat Wizard's gutters to board up the hole. And my best dress was somewhere in the rubble under my bed. I only had my old jersey and skirt. The Church Fête, in spite of a chilly wind, was full of people in their summer best, and

the first person we met
when we went through
the gate was Mrs Ward.
She was wearing a new
red dress and making her
new gold bracelet chink up
and down her arm by carrying a big bunch
of magic balloons which kept tugging to get away.
She smiled meanly at us.

"Come for your jumble, have you?" she said.
"I'm surprised you dare show your faces. You look
just like the two fools you are."

I'd admired Mrs Ward up to then. I was quite
disillusioned. Auntie May went dark red and we
both pretended not to hear. It was easy to pretend,
because the loudspeakers were making sounds like
a cat being attacked by bagpipes. We stalked past
Mrs Ward.

Usually Auntie May waits near the jumble stall
until the Fête is opened, so that she can be first
there; but this time we stalked past the jumble, and
the rifle range, and the lucky dip and then the
bowls pitch. There was a small white piglet in a
hutch to one side of the bowls. It kept pushing its
snout through the chicken-netting and getting stuck.

"Now, Cheryl!" Auntie May said, seeing me
looking.

But I could see the piglet was not clever like
Ranger and I was not interested this year.

Ranger was there, of course. He came pushing through the hedge as we were going to the flower tent. He gave me a friendly wink and trotted off into the crowd. A couple of ice-cream vans had arrived, and Ranger's plump white shape was here, there and everywhere, begging for ice-cream. Lizzie Holgate was there, handing money out in handfuls to all her six kids. All of them bought ice-creams with it and most of them gave theirs straight to Ranger. Auntie May snorted at the waste and we went round the flowers. The judges had already mysteriously been there and given First Prizes to all the wrong things. We stood in the hot, squashed grass looking at the Single Rose. Auntie May was feeling better by then.

"That, Cheryl," she said, "is the Way of Life. You have to accept it."

The Fat Wizard had won with a scrawny yellow rose. Old Ned had put in a perfect and wonderful red rose and hadn't won a prize at all. I didn't feel at all like accepting it.

All this time, the Vicar's voice kept coming over the loudspeakers saying, "One. Two. Three. Testing," mixed with howls and squalls. As we came out of the tent, he said "Ninety-nine!" followed by a noise like God eating celery and the band started to play outside the beer tent. The Fat Wizard's large shiny

Bentley was bumping slowly across the field towards the Vicar. Auntie May and I got quickly to the back of the crowd.

"I'm sure CRUNCH CHOMP needs no introduction from THUNDER CRASH," the loudspeakers said as the car stopped and George sprang out dressed as a chauffeur. "We are delighted SQUASH welcome CLATTER once again to TEA-TRAYS RUN OVER BY LORRY our little Fête."

George opened the door of the Bentley and the Fat Wizard climbed out. He was very angry again. He puffed and he glared and he panted, and he finally got both feet out on to the grass. They sank up to the ankles as soon as he took a step. The earth quivered. He took two more steps. Music stands in front of the band fell over. By this time the Fat Wizard was walking along a small trench, sinking lower every second. He must have weighed well over a ton. His bulging blue eyes flickered angrily about, looking for someone.

Auntie May said, in a mild, pleased voice, "I hope Tallulah Ward has the sense to keep out of sight."

But Mrs Ward was right near the edge of the crowd, easy to pick out by her red dress and the bunch of straining balloons. Her face was so pale that she had a bright red spot of make-up showing on each cheek.

Just then Lizzie Holgate came round the

Bentley, pushing her pushchair and surrounded by all her kids. They seemed to be looking for a good place to stand. Jimmy and Mary had to lift the pushchair over the trench the Fat Wizard had made, so that for a second the whole family was milling round the Fat Wizard.

When they moved on again, the Fat Wizard was the right weight. He climbed easily out of his trench and he took an easy step or so. But it never occurred to him to thank the Holgates. He just glared at Mrs Ward.

"If you'll just come over to the microphone, sir –" the Vicar called.

But Ranger had followed the Holgates round the Bentley, hoping for more ice-cream. He saw something was going on and he stood, looking about inquisitively. He looked at the Fat Wizard.

"Ah!" said the Fat Wizard. "Now I know what to do to that woman!" He pointed a fat finger at Mrs Ward, and he shouted out something that made an even louder noise than the loudspeakers.

All Mrs Ward's balloons went up together in a huddle, like hair standing on end. In place of Mrs Ward, there was suddenly a thin white pig with blobs of pink on its cheeks. It ran about among everyone's legs, trying to get itself out of its red dress. Then it dashed into the beer tent, trailing underclothes and squealing, and there was suddenly a lot of noise from in there too.

Everyone except Ranger looked at the Vicar, and the Vicar looked at the sky. Ranger looked at me – in a puzzled, reproachful way, as if he thought it was my fault that Mrs Ward was knocking tables over and squealing in the beer tent.

"Where do I stand to open this silly Fête?!" the Fat Wizard said.

"Oh no you won't open the Fête!" I screamed. I couldn't bear the way Ranger was looking. I rushed through the crowd and I stood in the open, with one hand stretched out towards the Fat Wizard and the other stretched towards Ranger. "You're selfish and greedy and cruel!" I yelled. 'Ranger would make a better human than you!'

The loudspeakers made a MOTORBIKE - STARTING - IN - HEAVEN noise. After that, Ranger and the Fat Wizard seemed to have changed places. The Fat Wizard was standing where Ranger had been, staring at me with amused piggy eyes. Where the Fat Wizard had been was a very fat pig with a sort of black waistcoat marked on its white skin. This pig had blue eyes and it looked stunned.

Jimmy Holgate shouted, "Cheryl! Look out!"

George was climbing out of the Bentley. His smart chauffeur's uniform burst off him.

He leapt towards me, towering over me, huge and blue-black. The tail he always seemed to be missing was lashing round his legs, thick and hairy, with a forked tip. I was terrified.

Lizzie Holgate and her kids arrived beside me. Auntie May was there too, holding her hat on dourly. And my mother was next to Auntie May, which did surprise me, because she never goes to the Church Fête. George towered and gnashed his long teeth. We all shouted "*Avant!*" and the loud-speakers went SCREAM POOP SCREAM and George vanished. The poor little piglet down by the bowling pitch suddenly went mad. George had possessed it. It screamed so hard that it almost drowned the noise in the beer tent.

Ranger winked at me. "Let's get this Fête open," he said to the Vicar in a pleasant grunty voice, "and we can all have an ice-cream."

But Lizzie Holgate was whispering to my mother, "Can you send her somewhere where there's no pigs around?"

Mother caught the glaring blue eye of the pig with the waistcoat. "Her Godmother. In Town," she whispered back.

I caught the two-thirty bus outside the gate. While the bus was turning round, Old Ned let the piglet out of his hutch and it chased after the bus, foaming at the mouth, until Jimmy Holgate managed to catch it by one leg.

I have never dared go back. Mother writes that the blue-eyed pig with the waistcoat is still roaming the woods, but they sent George to the bacon factory some time ago. Mother has Mrs Ward in the sty in her backyard. Even the Holgates can't turn her back. Ranger is still living at the Big House. He opens the Church Fête every year, and Mother says you couldn't have a nicer landlord.

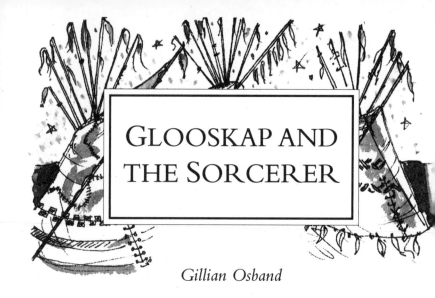

GLOOSKAP AND THE SORCERER

Gillian Osband

The Indians of North America have many stories to tell of the great magician and chief Glooskap. This is the story of Glooskap's battle with the sorcerer Win-Pe.

Glooskap lived with his tribe on a large island. In his wigwam lived an old woman, who he called "Grandmother", and a boy, Marten, who he called "Younger Brother."

The sorcerer, Win-Pe, also lived on the island, and as time went by he became more and more jealous of Glooskap, for Glooskap was a good magician who helped the Indians in times of trouble. The Indians loved Glooskap, for he was a wise and great magician and chief, but the more they loved him, the more Win-Pe hated him, and finally decided to get his revenge.

Win-Pe waited until winter was almost upon

them and Glooskap was away from the island. Then he crept up to Glooskap's camp with his men, tied up the old woman and the boy Marten, and carried them off with Glooskap's dogs. He also put out the fire, so that the magician would have no heat. Win-Pe knew that at times Glooskap had great magic power, but that at other times he had almost no magic at all. He knew that at that particular time, Glooskap's magic was at a very low ebb; and hoped that all alone on the island, without his dogs, his family and his fire, and without his magic, the magician would die during the bitter cold of winter.

Glooskap returned to his camp just as Win-Pe's canoes were out of reach. When the great magician saw what had happened, he raced down to the shore and called with his strength to his old grand-mother to try to set his dogs free, and get them back to him, for Win-Pe had been right: Glooskap's magic power was not with him at that time.

The old grandmother heard Glooskap's desperate call, and she made the dogs as small as mice, put them on a board of wood, and set them on the sea. The wind and the tide floated the wooden board back to the shore, where Glooskap stood alone.

For seven months Glooskap was alone on his island, slowly building up his magic power. At the end of seven months, he felt that his power was strong enough for him to set off and rescue his old grandmother and the boy, Marten. He stood on a large rock on the headland overlooking the sea, and, leaning on his bow, began to sing the magic song of the whales.

Before long, a small whale who had heard the magic song swam up to Glooskap. When he put his foot on the whale's back, the whale started to sink beneath the sea, for he was too heavy for him to carry; so Glooskap sent him on his way and sang the magic song again until a huge whale heard it, and swam to the rock where he stood.

Then Glooskap stood on its back, and the huge whale carried him swiftly across the oceans until they came to the shore of Newfoundland.

As they neared the shore the great whale started to become afraid, because the water was getting too shallow for it to swim safely. The whale called to Glooskap: "We are getting near the shore. Is the water still deep enough for me?"

And Glooskap answered: "The water is still deep. Swim on."

After the whale had swum a little further, it looked down and could see the shells on the ocean floor, and once again it called to Glooskap and asked fearfully: "Great chief, the land is near, and surely the water is too shallow for me to swim further."

But again Glooskap told the great whale that

the water was deep enough for him to swim safely, and instructed it to carry him with all speed.

So the whale swam on with great lashings of its tail to give it greater speed until, with one great thrust, it sped forward high onto the beach, and was stranded there just as it had feared.

Then the great whale cried out to Glooskap that it had carried him in total faith over the oceans, and had trusted him when he had said that the water was safe for him to swim through, and what had Glooskap done but betray him, and repay good with evil. The great whale knew that to be stranded on the beach meant certain death.

Glooskap jumped off the great whale's back and said to it: "Do not be afraid. I would never betray your trust or the good deed that you have done for me." And with one terrific heave, the great chief pushed the whale off the beach back into the deep water.

But the whale had been so terrified that it could hardly swim. So Glooskap said to it: "This is my gift to you for the service you have done me." And he took his magic pipe, filled it with tobacco, lit it, and gave it to the whale. As the whale smoked the pipe, its strength

returned and it was able to swim safely away from the dangerous shallow water.

From that time on, whenever a whale was seen to spout and blow, it was said to be smoking the magic pipe that Glooskap had given the great whale that had carried him so bravely from the island.

Then Glooskap set off in search of the evil sorcerer, Win-Pe, and his old grandmother and the young boy, Marten. Glooskap was a great tracker, and he was able to follow the sorcerer and his men by his knowledge of many small signs along the trail. And, whenever he could, Marten had left signs and signals for Glooskap to follow.

Win-Pe knew that when his magic returned the magician would follow him, and so he had sought the help of all the evil creatures along the way. Glooskap had to ward off and fight witches and fierce beasts. Win-Pe had even got the fearful stone giants to help him. But nothing was able to stop Glooskap as he followed the trail.

At last, one day, Glooskap came upon a camp where the embers of the fire were still warm, and he knew that, finally, he had caught up with his foe, for Marten had managed to leave his secret signs for Glooskap to see.

The secret sign was three lines with a crescent moon, so Glooskap knew that it would take three days to find Win-Pe's camp. Three days later, just as

Marten had marked, he came upon it.

Glooskap stayed hidden among the trees and waited and watched. At last he saw Marten leave the camp to gather wood for the fire. The boy looked thin and desperate. Glooskap waited until he was a safe distance from the camp, and then threw a small stick to attract his attention.

When Marten saw Glooskap he was overwhelmed with joy and relief, and would have cried out, but Glooskap managed to signal him in time to keep quiet, and to come closer to the spot where he was hiding without causing any suspicion.

When he was near enough, Glooskap whispered to him: "Tell Grandmother that I have found you, and then this is what you must do to help me defeat Win-Pe. When he sends you to fetch water, do as he says, but before you give it to him put in the water the worst filth you can find. Now go back to the camp before they become suspicious of your absence."

So Marten returned to the camp, and Glooskap crept nearer so that he could overhear and watch all that went on there.

In a short time, he heard Win-Pe call out angrily to Marten: "Marten, you lazy fool, bring me fresh water at once."

Marten went to fetch the water, and Win-Pe was then heard shouting at the old grandmother about the food she was cooking.

Marten brought the water for Win-Pe and meekly handed it to him. He had done as

Glooskap had instructed and put the worst filth he could find in the water, so that when Win-Pe took a mouthful of it, the taste was so foul that he spat it out, grabbed a burning log from the fire, and started lashing out at Marten.

In great fear the young boy ran away from the furious sorcerer, crying "Glooskap, my brother, save me, save me!"

"Cry out all you want for your brother," Win-Pe laughed nastily. "He can't save you! He is stranded on the island and is probably dead by now, and you shall join him!"

The sorcerer chased Marten through the trees. Glooskap had told Marten to do something that he knew would enrage Win-Pe; something that would so fill the sorcerer's mind with anger that his magic powers would be small, and possibly leave him altogether.

Seeing that his plan was working, the great chief emerged from behind the trees, and with all his power and goodness stood before his enemy, Win-Pe.

Win-Pe started back when he saw him, and tried to clear his mind of the great anger that was there and to regain his magic powers. But Glooskap, with all his magic strength, towered above him, so that Win-Pe seemed no more than a small evil dwarf. Then Glooskap stretched out with his bow and tapped Win-Pe on the head, and the evil sorcerer fell down dead.

So Glooskap, the great magician and chief, was re-united with his old grandmother, and his young brother, Marten. And the three of them wandered from camp to camp, and from tribe to tribe, where the great chief used his magic powers and his wisdom to bring help whenever it was needed.

LIZZIE DRIPPING
AND THE WITCH

Helen Cresswell

That day, Lizzie did not feel like walking back with the others after school. Becky Farmer called to her, but Lizzie pretended not to hear.

"Wants to play hospitals," she thought. "Sick of that game, I am. Only just got those spots washed off me she did with her felt-tips *last* time."

So she hung round, waiting to be the last to go, and thinking that perhaps she could walk along with Miss Platt.

"What is it, Lizzie?" asked Miss Platt, appearing behind her. "Have you forgotten something?"

"I was wondering if I could wait and walk along with you. I could show you that marrow I was telling you about – in Mr Briggs's garden. Honest, Miss Platt, it's the biggest I ever saw. I keep wondering if it's going to end up biggest there's ever been in the *world*. Going to put it in church

116

for Harvest Festival, he says, but rate it's going he won't get it in through't *door*!"

Miss Platt laughed, but not in the way some people might have laughed. A *proper* laugh, she had.

"Why, thank you," she said. "I'd love to see it, Lizzie, and you shall show it to me. But I have your books to mark before I go home. And I think Becky's waiting for you. I should go and play with her, outside, while the weather holds."

"Don't feel like it," said Lizzie. "Don't always feel like playing, you know."

"I know," said Miss Platt. "It's nice to be alone sometimes."

"Oh, I'm not *alone!*" cried Lizzie. "Least, I – oh, I dunno! 'Bye, Miss Platt!"

Becky Farmer beckoned to her as she went out through the school gate, but Lizzie shook her head and went in the other direction.

"Go home and get an apple or summat,' she thought, "and that book on giants, then I'll go to the Pingle, and sit and read under't beeches."

117

Patty was in the kitchen ironing.

"You, is it, Lizzie?" she said. "Nice day, was it?"

She said the same thing every day, and Lizzie often had the feeling that she never listened to the answer.

"Smashing," she said. "We did collage things, with leaves and nuts and that. Look!"

She held it up. It was all brown and gold and tattered – just *like* autumn, which was what it was supposed to be.

"Hmmm. Very nice. But don't leave it down here, Lizzie. It'll get sat on."

Lizzie held it up again. "Look, Dad!"

"That's real good, our Lizzie," said Albert, putting down his newspaper. "You've made a real pretty picture of it. Hang it on the wall, shall you?"

"Not in here, Albert, if you please," said Patty. "Clutter enough, without leaves on walls."

"Put it in your room, love, that's best," said Albert. "Look nice, that will."

"Till leaves start dropping off," said Patty tartly. The steam flew up out of the iron in clouds. "Till't leaves start dropping off and all over't floor for me to sweep up. Now nip up to't shop, Lizzie, will you, and fetch some butter."

"Bang go my giants," thought Lizzie. "Might've known."

"Here's money." Patty handed it over. "Look sharp now, Lizzie, we shall be wanting it teatime."

So Lizzie went up to the shop and bought the butter, and as she walked slowly back home down Kirk Street, she all of a sudden had the feeling that she would like a walk around the graveyard. And being Lizzie, it was no sooner thought than done. She scrambled up the bank by the memorial cross and next minute was through the little swing gate into the graveyard itself. She stopped dead.

You really could not believe your eyes. You could *not*, absolutely not, walk up your own street on a hot September afternoon, turn into the grave-yard for a quiet half-hour, and see a witch sitting there.

Lizzie saw the witch before the witch saw her. What the witch was doing, was sitting with her back propped against a tombstone – the one in memory of *Hannah Post of this parish and Albert Cyril beloved husband of the above 1802 to 1879 Peace Perfect Peace.* Lizzie was not sure which shocked her most – seeing a witch at all, or seeing a witch propped against a tombstone.

Nobody should sit, lean or stand upon a tombstone. It showed disrespect for the dead. Lizzie herself sometimes did all three of these things, but never *carelessly*, as if it didn't matter. When she sat on a tombstone, it was with a thudding heart and a pounding sense of wickedness that would have made it quite impossible for her to do a single row of knitting or read so much as a page of a book.

And the witch was doing both. She sat in a black, untidy heap with a book propped open against a little marble flower pot that Lizzie was sure had been moved from the nearby grave of *Betsy Mabel Glossop aged 79 years Life's Work Well Done.*

Her hands, which were the only part of her that showed, kept making awkward jerking stabs with a pair of long wooden pins from which hung a length of lacy, soot-black knitting. Either it was lacy, or full of holes. Holes, probably, Lizzie decided. The witch did not look at all a good knitter.

The longer she stood there, the more Lizzie wondered whether she was actually seeing what she seemed to be seeing. She closed her eyes for a moment, then opened them again. She saw the crooked stones, green with moss, she saw the tall cow parsley with its seeding heads, she saw the roof of Pond Farm in the dip below. And she saw a black bundle topped with a pointed hat propped against the tombstone of the Perfectly Peaceful Posts. She saw a witch.

Lizzie turned and went softly back along the little path by the church, through the gate and back into Kirk Street, hot and shadowless and smelling of the blue smoke from the burning stubble. No one was about except Jake Staples, who was not really worth talking to. He was playing marbles with himself outside his house. Lizzie stood over him for a minute, watching him cheat.

"Hello," she said. "Who's winning?"

"Me," said Jake.

It struck Lizzie that perhaps Jake was the one person in Little Hemlock who *would* believe there was a witch in the churchyard. After all, he had believed her the time she had told him his house was on fire. He had left off knocking conkers down from Mrs Adams's chestnut and gone running down the village like ten furies. (Leaving Lizzie, who often had a *reason* for fibbing, to pick up his pile of conkers and stow them in her own bag.)

"There's a witch in the graveyard," she told him now.

"And pigs can fly," replied Jake, killing two marbles in one go. "Cats've got five legs. Monkeys are bl–" (He was going to say 'blue'.)

"I tell you there is," she said.

"You go away, Lizzie Dripping," said Jake. "I'm busy."

"And don't you dare call me that!" she cried.

"Everyone else does. Lizzie Dripping! My ma says you're a fibber and I'm not to talk to you."

"You say that once more," said Lizzie, "and I'll kick your marbles flying. I'll kick them to the four corners of the earth!"

She liked saying that, because she knew for a fact that the earth was round and didn't *have* any corners. Jake began to pick his marbles up and stuff them rapidly into his pockets.

"I'm going to tell my ma about you," he said.

"And I'm going to tell that witch about you!" returned Lizzie.

She marched back towards the church. Once out of sight and past the gate, she tiptoed. It was one thing to see a witch, and quite another to let a witch see you.

There she still sat, in a great black hunch. Lizzie stepped off the path behind a particularly large, show-off slab in memory of one of *The Petersons of the Manor*. The soft buff plumes of seeding grass brushed her bare legs.

"I spy with my little eye!" said a voice.

Lizzie leapt and banged her knee hard against the stone.

"Owch!"

"Saw you the first time, and I see you now," came the same cracked, chatty voice. The fingers were still stabbing with the needles, the face still hidden under that wide black brim.

Lizzie stood poised. Should she run or should she stay? She wanted, despite the knocking of her knees and the thudding of her heart, to stay. She knew for a fact that in all Little Hemlock there was no one half so interesting to talk to as this witch.

"If *I* was going to hide," the voice went on, "I should vanish into thin air."

Lizzie stepped from behind the stone.

"What, knitting and all?" she asked, interested.

For answer, the witch vanished. Lizzie blinked. She could still smell clover and nettles, and the pigeons were still crooning in the yews, and at the far end of the village she could hear the chimes of the ice-cream van.

"I am definitely awake," she said to herself, and as if to prove it, stepped sideways and stung her leg on a nettle.

"Owch!" she cried again, rubbing it.

"So that's that," she said out loud at last. "Seeing one of my own fibs, I expect."

Lizzie was a very *honest* fibber.

Then the witch was there again, still knitting.

"You are there!" cried Lizzie.

"Knit one, slip one, knit one, pass the slip stitch over," said the witch. "Of course I am. And I'm fed up with knitting. Fiddling, baby clothes is. Fiddle fiddle fiddle."

She plunged the spare needle fiercely into the black cobweb, fished for the ball of wool, and stowed them all into a pocket somewhere in her black robes.

"The thing is," said Lizzie, choosing her words carefully. "There are no such things as witches."

"That's all right, then, isn't it?" said the witch. "Come a little closer, and I'll turn you into a toad."

Lizzie let out a little squeal and clapped her hand to her mouth.

"I'm sorry!" she cried. "I didn't mean to be rude!"

The witch looked up then. Her face certainly

looked like what a witch's face would look like if there were such things as witches.

"Try me," she said.

"T– try you?" repeated Lizzie.

"Tell me something to do. A test."

"You mean a *spell*?"

Lizzie felt a swift shiver under the hot sun. Could a spell happen in Little Hemlock, on her own doorstep?

"I – I don't know if I want to, actually, thank you," she said at last.

"Rubbish!" snapped the witch. "You're dying to, girl!"

It was true. The fibbing part of Lizzie, the part of her that wanted to believe in everything and anything under the sun, was itching. It was itching to see the impossible actually *happen*.

"Come along," said the witch. "I haven't got all day."

"Just a minute," said Lizzie. "Let me think."

Quick. Think. Blank. Nothing. The best fibber in Little Hemlock stuck for an idea. Lizzie Dripping, of all people!

"In a minute," said the witch, beginning to sound dangerous, "*I* shall think of something."

"Oh! Oh dear!" Lizzie was frantic. "What about . . . what about . . . ?"

125

She was hedging for time.

"What about what?" enquired the witch relentlessly.

"What–about–turning–that–bird–into–a–toad?"

It all came out in a rush. She didn't feel herself *think* it, only heard herself *say* it. Somewhere at the back of her mind she had the idea that witches specialized in turning things into toads. And if anything round here was going to be turned into a toad, she didn't want to be it.

"What? Is that all?" The witch sounded disappointed.

"Which bird?" She scanned about her with eyes that looked oddly short-sighted for a witch. As if reading Lizzie's thoughts (and a chill ran down Lizzie's back), she dug into her robes and fished out a pair of spectacles.

"Which bird?" she repeated, looking about her over the rims.

"Th – that one!" Lizzie really did not care. She picked on an unsuspecting thrush sitting halfway up a yew that hung over the grave of Robert Miller (*Come Unto Me All Ye That Labour*).

"Poor thrush!" she thought fleetingly, just in time to see it turn toad.

She clapped a hand to her mouth.

"Hmmmm!" she heard the witch's mutter. "Not much to *that*. Any more?"

She picked on a robin, worming by a granite cross.

"Oh!" Lizzie gasped again. "Poor robin!"

There were two toads now. One by the cross and one halfway up the yew. The one in the yew looked startled, even for a toad.

"Oh! Turn them back, can't you?" she cried. "Look at that poor thing up the tree – oooh! Look out – it's going to jump!"

It did, too. And what was even more surprising, landed safely. It certainly looked bewildered, staring out among the grasses on the grave of Robert Miller (*Come Unto Me All Ye That Labour*), but more at home than up in the tree.

"T'ain't nature, toads in trees," remarked the witch.

"For all the world," thought Lizzie, "as if turning birds into toads was nature!"

"Now what?" asked the witch impatiently.

"Now she's started spelling," thought Lizzie, "how on earth am I going to stop her?"

Desperately she racked her brains for something interesting but *safe*. After all, the witch had turned the birds *into* toads, but there was no guarantee at all that she would – or even could – turn them back again.

"P'raps I'd better find out," she thought.

"What about turning them back?" she suggested.

The witch looked disappointed.

"Back? Already? Bird to toad, toad to bird? Child's play. Waste a witch's time, would you?"

Sulkily she snapped her fingers again and muttered under her breath. Next minute the two surprised-looking toads were two surprised-looking birds. They flew off – right off and on out of sight. Lizzie watched them go – and hardly blamed them.

"Now what?" said the witch again. "And not toads, this time."

Lizzie's brain went blank again. Quick. Think.

"Don't believe in me girl, do ye?" snapped the witch. "*I* know. *I* can tell."

"Of – c–course I do!"

The witch sniffed.

"*My* turn, any hows," she said. "Turn and turn about. *My* turn to choose a spell."

"Oh – oh dear! All right, then!" cried Lizzie a little desperately. She crossed her fingers, on both hands.

"Now you see one!" cried the witch. "And now you see *three*!"

"Oooooh!" Lizzie let out a shrill squeal. Facing her in a row, like ravens on a bough, were *three* witches! Lizzie blinked rapidly, in case there was something in her eye that was making her see treble. But there was no doubt about it at all. Propped against the tombstone of the Perfectly Peaceful Posts were three definite, distinct witches.

Her own witch – the one in the middle – looked pleased.

"That's more like home," she remarked. "And three can spell easier than one, eh, girls?"

The other two cackled merrily.

"If all three of them do that spell," thought Lizzie in a panic, "then there'll be *nine* witches. And if *they* all do it, there'll be twenty-seven, and if *they* all do it, there'll be – " but her arithmetic gave out. Instead of a number, all she came up with was a terrible picture of Little Hemlock churchyard thick with spelling witches – *blackened* with them.

Lizzie was desperate. Her mother had told her time and again that she should never speak to strangers. But why, oh why, had she not warned her never, ever, to speak to witches?

"*Now* do you believe in witches?" cried Lizzie's witch triumphantly.

"I do! I do!" Lizzie cried. "I believed in you before, really I did! But now I believe in you *three* times as much! Honestly! Really!"

"Well, then," said the witch, "give us a spell to do. A proper one, this time. Come along, girl."

Lizzie Dripping's brain turned to water again.

"Speak up, girl!" snapped the witch. "I can't hear you!"

"I – I didn't say anything!" stammered Lizzie.

What should she say? Change church into a gingerbread palace . . . ? No. Put bags of potato crisps instead of daisies . . . ? Better . . . Make her own hair grow down to her waist and be butter-cup yellow instead of brown? *That* was it! Just as she'd always dreamed – two lovely long pigtails, long as Rapunzel's – or at least, long enough to

sit on. She would tie them with scarlet ribbons and parade up and down the Main Street. Wouldn't they all stare ...?

"I've thought!" she cried. "I've got a spell for you! Make my hair – "

But she never finished.

"Lizzie Dripping! Lizzie Dripping!"

She turned quickly. It was Jake Staples, there by the gate.

"Thought you said there was a witch!" he yelled. "Witch my foot! Witch my elbow! Witch yourself!

Lizzie Dripping, Lizzie Dripping,
Don't look now, your fibs are slipping!
Lizzie Dripping, Lizzie Dripping,
Don't l –"

"Go away!" she screamed. "Go away this minute! You'll spoil – "

She turned back to where the witches were, and stopped dead.

"Oooooh!" She let out her breath in a long gasp. Where the witches were – the witches weren't.

Gone. Vanished – as only witches *can* vanish. From one moment to the next, into thin air ....

"Lizzie Dripping, Lizzie Dripping!"

Jake was still calling, but she hardly heard him.

"Oh witch," she whispered. "Where are you?"

She stared at the tombstone of the Perfectly Peaceful Posts as if by staring hard enough, and long enough, she could *make* her reappear. Jake had stopped calling now, and there was no sound but for the purr of pigeons and the rustle of wind in the dry grasses.

Slowly, very slowly, she advanced.

"If she is still there – or if all three of them are still there, even if they are invisible, I might touch them . . . " she thought.

She paused. Gingerly she put out her hands, feeling the thin air. Nothing.

"That witch'nd me could've been friends," she thought.

Then very softly, she said out loud, "Goodbye, witch. I do believe in you, you know, even now

you're not here, and even though I don't know your name. And witch – " pause – "I'm coming back tomorrow. Will you be there . . . ?"

No answer.

"Goodbye, witch," said Lizzie Dripping. "Till tomorrow."

And she turned and went home, because in her money box she had ten pence, and she wanted to buy some scarlet ribbons . . .

A TALE OF
THREE TAILS

Charles J. Finger

Once, long ago, the rat had a beautiful tail like a horse, with long sweeping hairs, though it was before my time of life. It was in the days of old Hunbatz, and he was a wizard who lived in the dark of the great forest that used to be on the other side of the big river. In those days things were not as now and animals were different; some larger, some smaller. The deer had a tail like a dog, and the rabbit's tail was long and furry like the tail of a cat.

Now in that land there was a hunter with whom neither lasso nor arrow ever failed, and he had two sons, beautiful to look at and brave of heart, stout and quick of foot. Not only did the brothers work better than any men had ever worked, but they could play ball and sing, throwing the ball higher than birds could fly, and singing in a way that brought the wild things to hear them.

Nor was there living creature able to run as swiftly as the two brothers. The birds alone could out-race them.

The brothers being grown, their father thought that it was time for them to make a home for themselves, so chose a place on the farther side of the forest, and told them to clear it, which, he said, could be done in seven days. It was no little forest, you must remember, but a vast place, where sunlight never pierced, and the roots of trees were like great ropes; a jungle that stretched for miles and miles and the tangle in it was so thick that a monkey could barely get through without squeezing. Deep in the forest there was a blackness like the blackness of night. The trunks of the trees were so large that three men holding hands could not circle them and where there were no trees, there were vines and snake-like lianas and thorn bushes and flowers so great that a man could lie down to sleep in the shade of them.

The first day the brothers took a great space,

piling the trees at one corner, clearing the tangle and leaving all as smooth as the water of a lake. They sang as they worked, and they sang as they rested in the heat of the day, and the organ bird and the flute bird answered them from the gold-green shade. So pleasant was their music that the old iguana, though he was as big as a man, came from his resting place in the trees to listen.

Seeing how things were going, old Hunbatz in the dark of the forest grew very angry, fearing that his hiding place would soon dwindle and vanish. So he went to the great grey owl, his friend, and they talked the matter over between them. The owl told Hunbatz that he must set the father's heart against the brothers telling him that the boys were lazy and instead of working spent their time in playing with the ball and in singing.

"Go," said the owl, "to their father, and when he asks how the lads fare with their work, say to him:

They sing and they play
For half of the day.

It may fall out that he will grow angry and cut off their heads, and thus the forest will be safe for us."

That seemed to the wizard to be good advice, and before the close of the day's work, old Hunbatz, who could fly by flapping his hands in a certain way like a swimmer, cast himself into the air and flew with great swiftness to the place where the father lived. But he took care to dress himself like a woodman.

"Well met," said the father, seeing Hunbatz, but thinking him no wizard of course. "From where do you come?"

"From the other side of the forest," was the reply.

"Then perchance you saw my two sons who are clearing the forest," said the father.

"I did," said Hunbatz.

"And how are the boys doing?" asked the father.

At that old Hunbatz shook his head sadly and answered, as the owl had told him:

"They sing and they play
For half of the day."

That, you know, was quite untrue, for while they sang, there was no stopping of work, and as for the play, it is true that they threw the ball from one to the other, but so clever were they that one would throw the ball so high that it would take hours and hours before it came down again, and of course, while it was in the air, the brothers went on working.

"I would cut off their heads to teach them a lesson," said Hunbatz, "if they were sons of mine." Then he turned on his heel and went away, not flying until he was out of the father's sight, for he did not wish any man to know that he was a wizard.

To be sure, the good man was grieved and his face clouded, when he heard the tale of Hunbatz, but he said nothing, and, a short time after, the brothers came home. He was much surprised when, asking the lads how much work they had done that day, they told him that they had cleared off the space of forest he had bidden them to. After much thought he told them that the next day they would have to do twice as much as before. The brothers thought the new task hard, but they went to work with a good will and on the second day the trees fell like corn before a man with a machete, and before night they had finished that which they had been given to do.

Again old Hunbatz flew through the air to the father and tried to set him against the boys, and again that night, when the boys were home, their task was set for the next day twice as much as the day before.

It was the same the third day, and the fourth, until at last the boys came to a point where by the mightiest working they could not move a stick or a blade of grass more. And yet, because of old Hunbatz, the father set them a task still greater.

On the fifth day things looked very hopeless for the boys, and their hearts were sad as they looked at the forest and saw the task that their father had set them to do. They went to work feeling for the first time it would be impossible for the sun to go down on their finished task, and the heart of old Hunbatz was glad. But the birds in the forest were silent that morning, for they too knew that there were sad hearts in the brothers. Even the grasshoppers and the mosquitoes and the bees were still, and as for the boys, not a note of joy could they raise.

Then to them came the iguana, wise old lizard who knew everything that went on in the forest, and as soon as he had heard what the brothers had to say he smiled and called on them to listen, after making sure that there was no living creature to hear except the birds, for of them he had no fear, knowing that the birds tell no secrets.

"Be cheerful," said the iguana, "and I will tell you a charm. It is this: mark about the handles of your working tools rings of black, white, red and green, and before you start to work, sing:

I must do what I can,

Is the thought of a man,

and if your hearts are brave, you will see what happens."

Having said this and smiled on the brothers, the old iguana climbed into a tree and stretched himself along the branch of it where he could best see, and the birds gathered in a great circle, a matchless melody going up to the sky.

So the brothers took their axes, their spades, their hoes, and their machetes, and painted about the handles of them rings of black and of white and of red and of green, and their voices rang sweet and clear as they sang, as the iguana had told them:

I must do what I can,

Is the thought of a man.

No sooner had the last words passed than the whole company of birds broke out into a chorus, singing, chattering, chirping, whistling, screaming, each according to its manner and, without hands touching them, axes went to work cutting down trees, machetes chopped at lianas and vines, spades cleared and dug; and trees, bushes and weeds piled themselves in great heaps at the edge of the clearing, so that in less than an hour the whole task was done. Then it was that all things in the forest were glad and the good iguana smiled broadly. The very

monkeys joined in and, catching the ball which the brothers threw, tossed it from tree to tree until it passed through the whole jungle and back again.

But old Hunbatz was angry beyond measure, so angry that he whirled about on his heels three hundred times, turning so rapidly that he looked like a storm cloud, and his long whiskers were tangled about him like a mantle. But the faster he whirled, the more his anger boiled, and, flapping his hands, he shot into the air, going so swiftly that his very clothes were scorched.

"How are the boys?" asked the father, when Hunbatz stood before him.

For answer, Hunbatz screamed: "Your boys are idle fellows!

They sing and they play
For half of the day.

Had I such sons, I would cut their heads off to teach them a lesson."

Said the father: "Tomorrow I shall go to the forest, and if you have not spoken truth, then this arrow which has never yet missed a mark shall find one in your heart. But if it is as you say, then my sons shall feel my anger."

Old Hunbatz did not like that at all, for well he knew that the hunter's arrows were never wasted. So back he flew to the owl and the two of them whispered together. That night there was a great gathering of the animals: of the hare, the deer, the rat, the jaguar, the puma, the opossum and many others. The rat, the deer, and the rabbit led them, and in a wonderfully short time, not only were all things restored and the work of the day undone, but the trees and the bushes and the vines and the lianas that had been moved on the other days were put back in their old places, growing and blooming, so that all was as though the brothers had never been at the forest at all.

Sad was the hour the next morning when the hunter came with his two sons and saw the forest as though hand had never touched it. The brothers could not believe their eyes. Grinning from the thick of a rubber tree was the face of Hunbatz, and on his shoulder was the owl. For a moment the father thought to cut off the heads of the lads to teach them a lesson, but on second thought he told them that he would give them another chance.

"What should have been done is not done," he said. "I will grant you a day and a night to clear all the forest as you told me it was cleared. Tomorrow morning I will come again, and see whether all is well done." At that he left them and went his way.

No sooner had he gone than the two brothers went to see the iguana, who told them of the witchery of the owl and Hunbatz and bade them act as before. So they made the ring about the handles of their working tools once more and sang:

I must do what I can,

Is the thought of a man,

and, as on the day before, axes, machetes and spades went to work and in a short time all was clear again. Then the iguana told the brothers of the evil that Hunbatz had done and bade them set traps and keep watch that night. So three traps were made and set, and when night fell, from all parts of the forest there came animals led by the rat, the deer and the rabbit, and old Hunbatz and the owl watched from the dark caves of the leaves.

No sooner had the first three animals stepped into the clearing than they were caught fast in the traps, whereupon the rest of the animals turned and fled. Then the brothers rushed to the traps. The rabbit gave a great jump when he felt the jaws close upon his beautiful cat-like tail, but it was chopped off

close to the body. The deer, with his tail like a puma, fared no better. So both deer and rabbit fled to the woods ashamed, and, as you see for yourself, have had no tails ever since. As for the rat, he was far too wise to jump as the rabbit and deer had done. But seeing the brothers coming, he pulled and pulled and pulled so that all the beautiful hair was stripped, leaving him with but a bare and ugly thing of a tail as you see today.

The next morning when the hunter-father came, there was the forest cleared and all in good order as the boys had said. So he sought out old Hunbatz, who flapped his hands and flew for very fear. But so fast he went that his clothes were burnt off, and his skin was baked into a hard crust by the great heat, and he fell to the earth and so became what we call an armadillo. As for the two brothers, they lived very happily for many, many years, and things went well with them and the land they lived in was a land of good harvest and fruit trees.

So now you know the Tale of Three Tails and if you do not believe it, look at the rat and the deer and the rabbit and the armadillo, and see for yourself.

HAMISH AND THE WEE WITCH

Moira Miller

Hamish and Mirren, a newly-married couple, came home to their farm, all set to live happily ever after.

But sometimes things don't work out like that.

Mirren loved the little white house on the hillside. Every morning she ran out into the fields where the fresh taste of the sea mingled with the warm smell of the wild flowers. She laughed to see how the fat brown hens came running to greet her.

"Here, here. Chook chook chook," she called, scattering corn like golden rain from the big basket. The hens fussed around her feet pecking and squabbling as she called to them. The eggs they laid for Mirren seemed bigger and browner and the yolks more golden than ever before.

"Mmmmm, she's no' bad – for a laird's

daughter," sniffed Hamish's old mother. "But do you think she can milk a cow?"

Hamish laughed as he watched Mirren dance round the farmyard among the hens.

"Of course she can!" he said. "My wee Mirren can do anything." And he was just about right. Very soon Mirren was milking the cow as well and the big wooden bucket was filled to the top every day with rich creamy milk.

"You're a treasure," said Hamish, "and I would-na' change you for all the gold and silver in your father's kists."

Mirren laughed and went on about her work, singing like the thrush in the hawthorn bush. Even Hamish's old mother had to admit that the farm was a brighter and happier place.

It seemed as if it would always be like that, and they would live happily ever after but suddenly one day, there came a change.

Mirren stopped singing.

She came in from the byre after the morning milking with the big wooden pail only half full.

"Och, Mirren," said Hamish. "Is the wee cow not well?"

"I don't know," said Mirren, puzzled and upset. "She seems restless and unhappy, and though I begged for more that was all the milk she had to give."

"Well, never mind, Mirren," said Hamish.

"Maybe she'll do better in the morn, and if anyone can help her, you can."

But the next morning it was the same story. The wee cow only gave half a bucket of milk, and that so thin and weak it might as well have been water from the loch.

Mirren was very unhappy.

"No sense in crying over the milk," said Hamish trying to comfort her. "I'll see what I can do." That evening he took the bucket and went out to the byre.

As he stepped from the back door into the yard he was just in time to hear a scuffling sound, and catch a glimpse of a little old woman in a green cloak. In her hurry to leave she caught the cloak on a nail by the byre door.

"Whigmaleeries!" she hooted, and pulled at the cloth to free herself. As she did so Hamish could see that she was carrying a wooden pail. And that pail was full to the brim with rich creamy milk.

"Here!" called Hamish running after her. "That's

my milk you're after stealing." The little old woman whirled round and fixed him with a bright beady green eye.

"Away ye go," she croaked, pointing a finger like a twisted twig, "or I'll turn you into a toad!"

Hamish stepped back into the cottage and slammed the door shut as she vanished in a cloud of evil–smelling black smoke.

"We have to stop her," he said to his mother and Mirren as they sat down to supper later that evening. "But how?"

Mirren shook her head; she was at a loss to know what to do. Hamish turned to his mother. She was older and wiser and knew about these things.

"That woman is one of the Wee Folk," she said. "And it'll no' be easy to stop her, I'm thinking. But there is a way." She got up and looked quickly round the cottage – under the table, and up the chimney – then closing the door tight shut she came back and sat down.

"I've never tried it myself," she whispered, "but they do say that if you can find out the name of a wee witch then she'll have no power to cast a spell over you."

"Then we must find her name," said Mirren, "and send her back where she came from."

But that was not so easy. For days she and Hamish went round their neighbours asking if anyone knew of the old woman. They found that although she had stolen eggs from this one, and butter from that, nobody could help. They, none of them, knew who she was.

"We'll go down to Camusbuie," said Hamish. "There may be someone in the village who can help." But even old Biddy who kept the shop and knew all the gossip before it happened, was no help at all.

And every day the wee old witch came back to fill her bucket with stolen milk.

At last Hamish's old mother had had enough. She liked nothing better than the rich creamy milk with a plate of porridge and she was missing it very much.

She put down her spoon with a bang on the breakfast table. Hamish and Mirren jumped.

"I'll soon sort this out," she said. Pulling her shawl tightly round her she stamped out to the byre.

"Here, Mother!" shouted Hamish running after her. "She'll do something terrible!"

"Just let her try!" sniffed Hamish's mother. She slammed open the byre door, and there, sure enough, sat the wee old witch. She was perched on the old milking stool, rocking gently from side to side and crooning a strange song as she milked the wee cow into her big bucket.

"Out of there, you!" screamed Hamish's mother. "You can't even milk a cow properly. Look at the way you're doing it – all back side hindmost. No wonder the poor beast's upset!" She barged in knocking the old witch off her milking stool.

Hamish jumped back out of the way as she rolled over at his feet in a dirty green bundle.

"How dare you!" howled the old witch, her feet waving in the air. "I've been milking cows for three hundred and forty-nine years. Are you trying to tell me I don't know what I'm doing?"

"Just that," said Hamish's mother firmly. "Now get out of the way and let me get on with it."

The wee old witch staggered to her feet, her face purple with rage, her straggly hair stuck full of straw.

"I'll turn you into a toad!" she screamed, struggling to get up again.

"Aye, well, if you're as good at that as you are at milking, I'll not be too bothered," said Hamish's mother, calmly sitting down on the milking stool.

"Whigmaleeries!" shrieked the furious wee witch, gasping for breath. "I'll make you sorry about this. I will that! You'll live to regret this or . . . or my name's not – GRIZELDA GRIMITHISTLE!"

There was silence.

Hamish stared at his mother, who smiled and nodded.

"Grizelda Grimithistle is it? Well, well, fancy that," she said smugly.

Hamish roared with laughter at the sight of the wee witch's face.

"Much obliged to you for telling us, Grizelda

Grimithistle," he said. "And now that we know, you'll not be stealing any more milk."

"You can forget the eggs and butter from down the road too," said his mother.

The wee old witch was livid with fury. She screamed and stamped and spun round in such a temper that she rolled herself into a huge green ball. Still screeching and howling she whirled out of the byre and up over the hill, burning a path through the heather that is still there to this day.

Down in Camusbuie they said afterwards that her howls could be heard clear across the Seven Glens and the echoes rolled like thunder round the top of the Ben of Balvie all that day.

"I don't doubt we've seen the last of Grizelda Grimithistle on this farm," said Hamish's old mother as she picked up the bucket full of rich creamy milk for her porridge.

And so they had – well, almost.

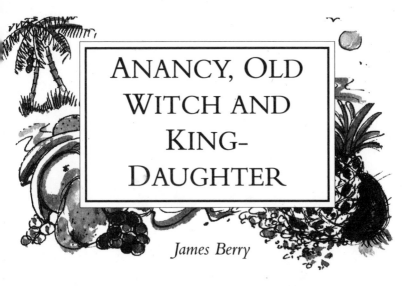

ANANCY, OLD WITCH AND KING-DAUGHTER

James Berry

From the day King-Daughter is born, King-Wife decides she'll keep her girl child's name a secret. King-Wife sees that if her daughter's name isn't known, guessing it will be a test for the man who wants to marry her when she grows up. King-Wife smiles to herself saying, "Yes, that will be good. That will make him show how clever he really is. The first one – the first one who guesses her name – shall marry my daughter."

All servants at the palace become well warned. "Tell no one Daughter's name."

Every servant swears on oath. "Never ever will I let Daughter's real name come from my lips to anyone outside this big and beautiful palace."

King-Daughter is to be talked about only as "Daughter".

Then one day everybody begins to talk.

"King-Daughter is old enough to marry." "What?" "Yes, yes, yes! King-Daughter is old enough to marry."

From everywhere, rich and famous young men begin to go in their carriages to the palace, to guess King-Daughter's name.

When Anancy hears what is happening, Anancy becomes excited. Anancy walks up and down saying to himself, "Bro Nancy, you have a chance. You know you have a good-good chance to marry King-Daughter."

Anancy goes to see Bro Dog.

"Bro Dog," Anancy says, "suppose – just suppose – you and me should play a game, could you be a first-class partner?"

"Bro Nancy," Dog says, "you know very well I'm never second class. Whatever I agree to I agree to."

"Well," Anancy says, "how smart a bad man beggar can you be?"

"A bad man and a beggar together?"

"I think I'm thinking like that," Anancy says.

"I can try," Dog says. "I can try."

Anancy dresses Dog. Anancy works on Dog till Dog looks like a scabby, ragged, dirty and smelly beggar.

"Bro Dog," Anancy says, "oh, you look perfect."

"Perfect what?" Dog says.

"Perfectly awful. Perfect bad man beggar to be scorned, hated, despised."

"What?" Dog says. "Suppose I get hurt?"

"Bro Dog, all the time, we'll be together," Anancy assures him.

Dog and Anancy take a short cut and come to a famous royal picnic spot. They both hide themselves behind bushes. Palace servants arrive ahead by themselves. They spread cloths and mats on the grass, put out picnic baskets together and sit awaiting the royal party.

Bro Dog creeps up behind the backs of the servants. He snatches the prettiest cloth, with DAUGHTER embroidered on it, and begins running about with it. Furious, the servants leap up and rush at Bro Dog.

"Drop it," they demand. "Nasty old mangy dog, drop it. Drop the cloth!" Dog rushes about playfully and then attempts to run away with the cloth. A royal maid runs after Dog. Really wild, she shouts, "Mangy dog, drop Princess Basamwe's picnic cloth!" Dog immediately drops the cloth and runs away.

All the way home, Anancy sings:
"Nobody knows her name.
Nobody knows her name.
Then who is Princess Basamwe?
Who is Princess Basamwe, O?
Princes Basamwe, Basamwe, Basamwe."

Anancy becomes determined not to make any mistakes. It seems most important to Anancy that he should go and see Old Witch. But Old Witch needs money. Where can he get money?

Anancy remembers where money is. He goes and steals a gold piece from Bro Monkey. What Anancy doesn't know is that Monkey keeps the pile of gold pieces in the cave for Old Witch.

Anancy goes to see Old Witch in her plain

earth-floor thatch-house. Old Witch sits
surrounded by Snake, Alligator and a long leg
Jumby Bird. Old Witch doesn't ask Anancy to sit,
only to put down his piece of gold. Old Witch
notices the gold but doesn't say she knows it comes
from her own pile of gold pieces.

Old Witch works her tricks with Anancy. She
tells him a certain time when he should start out
for the palace. She tells him he'll find himself suited
out with everything, at that certain time.

At that certain time next day Anancy can't believe
his good luck. He suddenly finds himself dressed like
a prince – perfect-perfect. He steps out of his door.
And there a horse and carriage awaits him.

Carrying gifts, Anancy arrives at the palace in
his shining open-top carriage. Anancy looks everything of a best-dressed prince. He stands proud-
proud in his carriage at the palace gate and begins
to sing:

"Nobody knows her name.
Nobody knows her name.
Then who is Princess Basamwe?"

As Anancy calls the name Basamwe the palace gate swings open wide. Anancy's carriage drives up to the palace door. He stands in his carriage and sings:

"Nobody knows her name.
Nobody knows her name.
Then who is Princess Basamwe?
Who is Princess Basamwe, O?
Princess Basamwe, Basamwe, Basamwe."

The King, King-Wife, King-Daughter and the whole royal family come out on the big veranda. As the stare of King-Daughter's eyes touches Anancy, his horse and carriage vanishes. King-Daughter blinks; Anancy's top hat vanishes. She blinks again; his shoes vanish. She blinks again; his jacket, then his watch and chain, his walking stick, his trousers, all vanish. As he's going to be naked he finds himself standing in his own ordinary clothes, clutching his gifts of silver sandals, necklace and headdress. Anancy turns into spider and disappears.

Anancy hurries back to Old Witch.

Hurrying along, in his ordinary clothes again – without princely carriage, without princely dress – Anancy says to himself, "Oh well, nice things come, nice things go. Even day comes, day goes, like magic." But Anancy knows that somehow his stolen gold piece given to Old Witch has made her cross. Her angry spell has stripped him. Yet Anancy reminds himself, "Old Witch has done something. She's done something. She'll have to do another something!"

Anancy comes into Old Witch house and again stands on her plain earth-floor. Snake, Alligator and Jumby Bird are there with Old Witch. Before Anancy can open his mouth to speak Old Witch speaks. Not even looking at Anancy, Old Witch says, "Go and hand your gifts to the first three women you meet. Go, as I say."

Anancy leaves. And one after the other, Anancy gives away his gifts to women he meets, as Old Witch says. And, something the least expected happens.

The woman he hands his last-last gift to becomes Anancy's wife.